P9-DWK-547

A- ⚒   H- ⬎   S- ◿
D- ⊒   I- 🦅   T- ⬐
E- ⟓   L- ▢   W- ⊨
G- ▢   N- ⬬   Y- ⟑
R- ▭

THE AIR SEEMED TO
WHISPER THAT THE PAST
WAS VERY MUCH ALIVE. . . .

BEYOND THE GRAVE

THE 39 CLUES

JUDE WATSON

SCHOLASTIC INC.

NEW YORK TORONTO LONDON AUCKLAND SYDNEY
MEXICO CITY NEW DELHI HONG KONG BUENOS AIRES

For Cleo, my partner in adventures.
This one is for you.

— JW

All rights reserved. Published by
Scholastic Inc., *Publishers since 1920.*
SCHOLASTIC, THE 39 CLUES, and associated logos
are trademarks and/or registered trademarks of Scholastic Inc.

Library of Congress Control Number: 2008941383

ISBN-13: 978-0-545-09061-2
ISBN-10: 0-545-09061-X

10 9 8 7 6 5 4 3 2 1   09 10 11 12 13

Book design and illustration by SJI Associates, Inc.

Library edition, June 2009

Printed in China

Scholastic US: 557 Broadway • New York, NY 10012
Scholastic Canada: 604 King Street West • Toronto, ON · M5V 1E1
Scholastic New Zealand Limited: Private Bag 94407 • Greenmount, Manukau 2141
Scholastic UK Ltd.: Euston House • 24 Eversholt Street • London NW1 1DB

CHAPTER 1

If Amy Cahill had to list what was wrong with eleven-year-old brothers, their habit of disappearing would be *numero uno*.

Or maybe the fact that they existed in the first place.

And then there was the whole burping the alphabet thing. . . .

Amy stood in the middle of the Khan el-Khalili market in Cairo, her head swiveling frantically, trying to find her brother, Dan. The blur of jet lag was interfering with normal brain function. Dan had just been at her side a moment ago. Then she turned for *two seconds* to buy a Nefertiti pencil, and when she turned back, Dan was gone.

The air was thick with heat and music and the calls of shopkeepers. Bright banners waved overhead. Tourists weaved through the streets, wearing their backpacks on their chests to safeguard against pickpockets and stopping to take pictures every few minutes. A woman in a head scarf dodged a row of turquoise chairs to follow after her two boys. A man with a crate full of oranges balanced them on his head with one hand. A tourist in a baseball cap and a T-shirt proclaiming I WANT MY MUMMY strolled past Amy, her camera held up in front of her face.

Amy felt the heat like waves against her skin. She hoped she wouldn't faint. Colors swarmed, faces dissolved, unfamiliar noises pounded against her ears. She had never liked crowds, and Cairo seemed like the city that had invented them.

She turned, her hand on her waist pack. Their au pair, Nellie Gomez, was just down the alley, bargaining over spices. Amy could just catch a glimpse of her crazy half-blond, half-black hair.

Less than an hour ago, they'd been in a taxi, riding into Cairo from the airport. Then when the cabdriver had casually pointed out the window and said, "The Khan market starts here, very good place," Nellie had suddenly yelled, "Stop!" Before they knew what was happening, they'd landed in the market with luggage and cat carrier. Saladin had meowed furiously when Nellie promised, "Just ten minutes, that's all I need, and then we'll go straight to the hotel. . . . Cool! Cardamom pods!" For Nellie, every new city was just another opportunity for weird food.

Finally, Amy spotted Dan through the crowd. He was pressed against a shop window crowded with souvenirs. She had a feeling he was captivated by the King Tutankhamen pencil sharpener, but it could have been the flashlight in the shape of a mummy.

As she crossed the alley, Dan kept appearing and disappearing through the meandering crowd. The hot sun was blinding. She hoped that air-conditioning was in her future.

The tourist in the I WANT MY MUMMY T-shirt drifted closer to Dan. She pushed her white sunglasses down her nose. Some small alarm chimed inside Amy. A man in a straw hat blocked her view, and she dodged to one side.

The tourist bent her index finger back at the first joint, as if she had a cramp. The hot sun glinted on something protruding from her nail.

"Dan!" Amy screamed. The music and the calls of the shopkeepers — *Five dollars, five dollars!* — drowned her out. She darted past a man balancing a dozen neon-colored soccer balls in a net.

The hypodermic needle protruded out of the tourist's clawlike finger. Dan leaned closer to the window. . . .

"Dan!" She screamed the name. In her head. But it came out like a strangled croak.

Amy threw herself forward. At the very last second, she flung out her hand. The needle jammed into the Nefertiti pencil and stuck.

For one swift second, all Amy could do was stare down at the glint of sunlight on metal. In slow motion, a drop of something lethal fell from the tip and hit the dust.

Amy looked into the face of Irina Spasky. Former KGB agent. Spy. Cousin.

Irina's left eye twitched. *"Blin!"* She twisted her hand, but the needle remained stuck in the pencil.

The shopkeeper hurried over. "Beautiful lady, it is stuck on you. Here, I have more pencils for you!"

Irina turned on him fiercely. "I don't want your fancy pencils, shopkeeper of things!"

Amy and Dan didn't wait another second. Dan moved like a midfielder through the crowd, and Amy followed in his wake.

Legs pumping, they ran until their lungs burned, dashing through the maze of twisting alleys. Finally they stopped, bent over at the waist, and tried to catch their breath. When they looked up, Amy realized they were lost. Badly, stupidly, irredeemably lost.

"Nellie will be looking for us," Amy said. She flipped open her cell phone. "No signal. We'll have to find our way back."

"And hope we don't bump into Comrade Irina," Dan said. "I can skip the family reunion."

By now they were used to meeting family members with mayhem on their minds. Just weeks ago they'd had a hard time coping with the fact of their grandmother's death. After their parents died, Grace had been the most important person in Amy and Dan's life. Even though they didn't live with her, they spent weekends at her mansion outside of Boston, and she always took them for trips during the school year and in the summers. Grace's death from cancer knocked them off their feet.

But that had been only the first of many shocks to come.

Grace had invited the four branches of the Cahill family to the reading of her will. Appearing on a video, she'd offered them a choice. Take a million dollars and walk away or join in a chase for 39 Clues and become the most powerful person in the world. Even though the million had seemed like one sweet deal, Amy and Dan hadn't really hesitated. They knew Grace would want them to accept the challenge. For Grace, there was no such thing as the easy way out.

The decision had been easy. It was the living up to it that was hard. In her old life, Amy had thought *playing to win* was Courtney Catowski spiking a volleyball on her head. Now she knew what competition was really about. Relatives like Irina played for keeps. She'd drug them, kidnap them, even kill them if she had to.

They started to walk. Amy felt as though they were going in circles. Like in a dream, where you run and run and get nowhere. Yesterday she'd been in Seoul, Korea. Before that, Tokyo and Venice. Vienna and Salzburg, Austria. Paris. Philadelphia. She'd even touched down on a private airfield in Russia.

She'd never had so many secrets before.

She'd never imagined she could be so afraid.

She'd never imagined she could be so brave.

Just a few days ago in Seoul they'd nearly been buried alive. Left for dead by people she trusted. Natalie and Ian Kabra . . . she wouldn't think about him. Wouldn't think about how he held her hand and told her that together they could form a great alliance. The alliance lasted a couple of hours, until he saw the opportunity to leave her for dead.

Wouldn't. Think. About. Ian.

Then they discovered that the only family member they almost-trusted, their uncle Alistair Oh, had double-crossed them as well. Pretended to be dead when he was clearly very much alive.

What had sent them hurtling through international air space to Cairo was a hint, no more than that. But they were used to grabbing on to hints and riding them for all they were worth. A pyramid shape and a word. Sakhet. The Egyptian goddess with the lion's head. Amy had bought several books before they left Korea and researched the goddess, but she still didn't know why they were sent here . . . or what, exactly, they were looking for.

Amy felt sweat trickle in rivers underneath her T-shirt. The temperature was over ninety. Her hair was sticking to the back of her neck. She thought of Ian, who no matter what the circumstances always looked so cool.

Wouldn't. Think. About. Ian.

The noise pressed against her ears, an exotic, whirling cacophony of horns honking, vendors shouting, cell phones ringing, and someone yelling over it all, "Move it, lame-o!"

Oh. That voice was not so exotic. It was Dan.

"Russian spy at two o'clock and gaining!" he hissed.

Irina hadn't seen them yet. She was too busy looking for them. She prowled along the opposite side, peering into shop windows.

Amy pulled Dan into a café. Men sat at tables, drinking tea and having murmured conversations or reading newspapers. Tourists sat with their guidebooks over glasses of juice. As Amy squeezed past, her bulging backpack slammed against a burly gentleman sitting with a glass of mint tea. The tea spilled on his white suit.

Every eye in the café turned to Amy. The *clackety-clack* of a backgammon game stopped. She felt her face turn bright red. She hated being the center of attention at any time, and especially when she'd done something clumsy.

"S-s-sorry!" Amy stammered. Her stutter came out when she was nervous, and she hated it. She tried to mop up the mess.

"It's fine, young lady, do not worry." The man smiled kindly at her and waved to the waiter. "It is just tea."

On the walls, heavy antique mirrors reflected the scene. Amy saw her own red face, her fluttering hands, the eyes of the patrons . . . and the door opening. Even the tourist attire and white plastic sunglasses couldn't disguise the way Irina soldier-marched into the café, as if she were inspecting everyone in it for demerits.

And in exactly three seconds, her gaze would land on them.

CHAPTER 2

The fat man stood up, giving them cover for an instant. Dan grabbed the chance. He dodged behind a thick curtain, pulling Amy after him.

They found themselves in a short hallway that led to a side door. They dashed outside.

Now they were in an even smaller alley that snaked behind the shops. They knew Irina would be out there in a matter of seconds. They dodged a cart piled high with crates and a surprised man sleeping in the sun. Seeing a back door to a shop, they ran through it into a storeroom. It was dark and dusty, and Dan started to wheeze.

"Use your inhaler," Amy said.

"It's . . . in . . . Nellie's . . . carry-on," Dan got out. He hated this feeling. As though someone were squeezing his lungs. It happened at the worst times.

"Good place for it. Come on."

Amy quickly led Dan out of the dusty storeroom and into the store. It was bright and airy, with spangled belly dancing costumes hanging from the ceiling.

"Welcome! You are looking for lovely costume? I'll give you a deal!"

"Not my color! But thanks!" Dan called as he ran out.

Down another twisting street, then another. Finally, Amy ordered a halt.

"We lost her."

"For now." Dan grabbed her elbow. "Amy, look."

Only a few feet away, they saw a sign: S A K H E T

In the dramatically red-curtained window, a statue stood alone. Blue stone, with a lion's head, standing tall and proud.

Amy and Dan looked at each other. Without a word, they pushed into the shop.

They made a beeline for the Sakhet statue. It was obviously very old. The surface was worn and one of the lion's ears had cracked off.

The shop owner hurried forward, a thin, eager man in black pants and a white shirt. "You are interested? She is beautiful. Authentic, not a replica. Once owned by Napoleon," the man went on. "You have an excellent eye."

"Napoleon? Isn't that an Italian pastry?" Dan asked. "Sort of gooey inside?"

Amy rolled her eyes. "You're the one with goo — for brains. Napoleon was the French emperor. Remember, he conquered the world? We saw a picture of him in the Lucian stronghold back in Paris? He's a Cahill. One of our ancestors."

The Lucian branch of the Cahill family had a strategic sense that was amazing. Of course, their powers had dwindled down to the petty, nasty deeds of Ian and Natalie Kabra and the crazy Russian Irina Spasky.

"If he'd picked out this Sakhet, it could be important," Dan said.

"It can't be this easy," Amy said.

"Why not, when everything else has been so hard?" Dan pointed out.

The shopkeeper raised his voice, trying to get them back again. "I see you are fascinated. Yes, Napoleon owned many treasures. Some went back to France, some stayed here." He put his hand on the statue and caressed it. "Are your parents with you? I'll give you the best price. I have the premier shop in Cairo."

"No, thanks," Dan said. Back home, he was a collector. He knew the best way to bargain was to pretend you didn't care. "Come on, Amy. Let's keep looking. Why would Napoleon have stuff in Egypt, anyway?"

"Napoleon invaded Egypt in 1798," Amy said.

"Ah, the young lady knows her history. I would be so proud if this statue came into her brilliant hands. Here." He gave her the statue.

It felt strange to touch something so old. Something Napoleon had touched. Every so often she got a deep thrill from a sense of her own DNA linking like a chain down a line leading to a bunch of extraordinary people. Napoleon!

"Only two thousand," he said.

Amy jumped. "Two thousand *dollars*?"

"For you, fifteen hundred. Someone from the Cairo Museum is interested in this piece. He is coming back at four o'clock."

"I doubt that, Abdul."

Amy turned. She'd noticed the tall, blond stranger browsing at the other part of the store. She hadn't noticed him draw closer. He was in his twenties, dressed in a T-shirt, khaki shorts, and sandals. His eyes were vivid green next to his tan.

"Unless he's looking for a trinket for his key ring," he said in a British accent.

He plucked the Sakhet from her hands. "I'd date this piece at . . . maybe 2007?"

"Really, Theo, you are mistaken," the shopkeeper said, smiling uneasily. "This is authentic, I assure you —"

"Assurances aside, I think you're trying to take these two youngsters for a ride on the fake artifact express," the man named Theo said.

"He said Napoleon had owned it," Dan said.

"Maybe," Theo said. "Joe Napoleon down the street runs a great Italian restaurant."

"I *told* you Napoleon was Italian," Dan said scornfully to Amy.

"Actually, he was born in Corsica," Theo said. "Would you kids like to see the rest of the shop?"

"No need," Abdul said quickly. "I see I don't have what you want. Perhaps next door you'll find what you're looking for. It's time for my tea break, so . . ."

Theo strode past him and pushed open a heavy curtain. At a long table, several workers were hunched over. Amy stood on tiptoe as the shop owner tried to block her view. The workers were using wire brushes and sandpaper on a row of statues similar to the Sakhet. They were sanding and brushing them in order to make them look old.

Abdul shrugged. "Hey, it's a living."

"No harm, no foul," Theo said.

Just then Dan grabbed Amy's arm. Peering through the window and shading her eyes was Irina.

Theo had noticed their alarm. "Who's that? Your mother?"

"Someone on our tour. She's a total pain," Amy said.

"Always following us," Dan said. "Is there another way out of here?"

"One thing you should know about me," Theo said. "I *always* know the back way."

The brass bell on the front door jangled as they pushed through the curtain and made their escape.

This time it was easier. All they had to do was follow Theo. He moved quickly and expertly through the maze of narrow alleys. Finally, they stopped to rest near the arched entrance to the market.

"I think you're safe," Theo said. "Can I get you a taxi back to your hotel?"

"We lost our au pair," Dan said. "We'd better find her. Uh, where are we?"

"Let's start with this. Where did you leave her?"

Amy frowned. "By some spices?"

"Okay, that narrows it down somewhat. Can you remember anything else?"

Dan closed his eyes. "A yellow sign with maroon letters in Arabic. Three rows of spice baskets, nuts in green buckets. Shopkeeper with mustache and a mole on his left cheek. Next door was a fruit stall, thin guy in a red hat yelling, 'Pomegranates!'"

Theo cocked an eyebrow at Amy. "Is he always like this?"

"Constantly."

Again they followed Theo through the market, keeping a careful eye out for Irina.

"Do you live here?" Amy asked him as they weaved through the crowds.

"Went to university in England but came back and haven't left since."

"You sure know your way around," Amy said.

"I used to be a tour guide," Theo said. He smiled at her, and Amy suddenly realized that he was seriously good-looking.

A fuming Nellie stood outside the stall where they'd left her. A string bag stuffed full of packages swung from her wrist. Dan's duffel was at her feet, and her own bag, plus the nylon tote they'd borrowed from Alistair, was piled on top. Saladin the cat meowed woefully in his cat carrier. She advanced on them furiously.

"Where have you been? I thought you were kidnapped!" Suddenly, Nellie caught sight of Theo. She stopped short. She gave Theo a long look, from the top of his blond head to his suntanned toes. "Well, hel-lo, Indiana Jones," she purred in a voice just like Saladin made when he caught sight of a filet of red snapper in his food bowl.

Since they'd left her, Nellie had gone shopping. Over her black T-shirt was a gauzy lavender fabric that she'd wound around her body to make a tunic. Black kohl now rimmed her eyes, and beaded bangles slid up her arm from wrist to elbow. Gold dusted her eyelids. She looked as though she were about to run off to a hip-hop harem.

"Well, hello, Mary Poppins," Theo replied with a grin.

"How astute. I'm practically perfect in every way," Nellie said. She stuck out her hand. "I'm Nellie Gomez."

"Theo Cotter."

Dan rolled his eyes as Nellie's hand stayed in Theo's longer than a handshake should take. Did Nellie actually *blush*? He didn't think she was capable of it.

"Theo saved us from buying an ancient priceless artifact that was made yesterday," Amy said.

Theo shrugged. "Unfortunately, you happened to stumble into one of the worst tourist traps around. I can show you some of the more authentic shops if you'd like," he said, his eyes on Nellie.

"That would be amazing," Nellie said, as if Theo had just offered to show her the secrets of the universe.

"I think we'd better get to our hotel," Amy said. Theo seemed okay, but why should they trust him? Besides, they didn't have time to waste. Before they'd left Seoul, they'd found a frequent-traveler's card in Alistair's bedroom. Dan had pocketed it and they'd used it at the airport to book a room at a hotel called the Excelsior. Amy was anxious to check in and figure out their next step. This was all happening too fast.

Theo took a couple of Nellie's bags from her. "You're interested in Napoleon, right?" he said to Amy. "Did you know that when he invaded Egypt he brought scholars and archaeologists and artists with him to study the country?"

Well, isn't that sooo Lucian of him, Dan thought.

"The house where his scholars lived is a museum now. I know the curator there."

Uh-oh, Dan thought. As soon as his sister heard the word *museum,* she started to salivate. It was like waving a double-fudge brownie in front of her face.

"Is it nearby?" Amy asked eagerly. Maybe she should rethink this. If the house was still there, they might be able to find something to lead them to a Clue.

"Nothing is too far in Cairo," Theo said. "Sennari House. It's just over on Haret Monge."

"Right. We knew that," Dan said.

"Come on, I'll get us a taxi."

Theo turned and led the way to the frenzy of a downtown street. If there were lanes on the wide street, Dan couldn't see them. Cars slithered into tiny spaces, cut off trucks, accelerated at red lights, and tailgated buses, all to a symphony of horn blowing and yelling. Amy, Dan, and Nellie exchanged glances. They couldn't imagine how to find a taxi in the melee.

Theo stepped calmly out into the street, held up a hand, and a taxi skidded to a stop.

"You see?" Nellie said in awe. "He *is* Indiana Jones."

CHAPTER 3

When they arrived at Sennari House, Theo tossed a bundle of bills at the driver and spoke a few words in Arabic. "Baksheesh," he told them.

"Gesundheit," Dan said.

Theo grinned. "No, baksheesh means a tip. Now he'll wait for us."

Theo moved ahead to walk with Nellie, and Dan turned to Amy.

"Not that I'm not really excited about going to yet another museum, but what exactly are we looking for?"

"I don't know," Amy admitted.

"This connection to Napoleon seems a little . . . uh . . . random."

"I know. It's not much to go on. But we didn't have much to go on in Philadelphia, Paris, Vienna, Salzburg, Venice, Tokyo, and Seoul. We still managed to find clues. We know Napoleon was a Lucian. We think there is a clue in Egypt. So if he found it, or if he found *something,* he might have left a hint here for the Lucians."

"It *would* be fun to steal something out from under Comrade Irina's nose," Dan admitted.

Theo insisted on buying their tickets. They passed through a small door and into a courtyard. Small date palms and red-flowered bushes created a cooling effect despite the lack of shade. A fountain sat in the center.

"Sennari House was built in 1794," Theo explained. "It's an example of classic Islamic domestic architecture, built around a central courtyard, called a *sahn*. I believe it has some of the most beautiful *mashrabeya* screens in Cairo."

"Those are the carved wooden screens in the windows," Amy explained, pointing.

"Napoleon's scholars created Egyptology for the West," Theo said. "After their writings were published, it started a craze all over Europe for everything Egyptian."

"That's fascinating," Nellie said.

"I'm on the edge of my seat," Dan said. Nellie stepped on his foot.

"They used to have a permanent exhibition of Napoleon's personal collection long ago, but it was removed in 1926," Theo explained. "The building was renovated back in the 1990s. Now they have some fine examples of textiles and ceramic art."

Dan held on to the end of Amy's T-shirt so she couldn't follow the two as they moved off. If he didn't stop her, Amy would spend hours in a dusty, old museum, sopping up completely useless information.

"Dude, we have work to do," he told her. "Where should we start?"

"I guess just wander around and look at the stuff that seems original," Amy said.

"Okay, not much of a plan, but it's a plan."

They explored all over the building, but it was hard to tell what was absolutely original to the structure and what had been repaired or renovated. Finally, they found an old stone staircase leading back down to the courtyard.

"The Lucians are all little Napoleons," Dan grumbled. "Look at Ian and Natalie. Just a couple of smarty-pants with cash. Comrade Irina? A smarty-pants with a tic. Napoleon? He was a smarty-pants with an army."

"Thanks, professor, for that illuminating lecture on the Napoleonic Wars," Amy said. "Look at those carvings! Theo was right. These screens are amazing. And look at these gorgeous tiles," Amy said, running her hand along the wall.

"You sound like Ian Kabra. Remember when he admired Alistair's window moldings?" Amy's face fell. Oops—he'd mentioned *the name*. Every time he let it slip, Amy got that *boo-hoo my hamster died* look on her face. Amazing that a fourteen-year-old, close-to-normal girl could fall for such a serious creep. He'd thought—well, he'd *hoped*—that a sister of his would be cooler than that.

Amy's lost look suddenly changed to curiosity. She pointed to a tile. "Doesn't that look familiar?"

Dan squatted down. "It's the Lucian crest!" The crest was hidden within the design, but he recognized it. "It's the only one like this."

"This has got to be some kind of hint!" Amy said excitedly. "Maybe there's something behind it." She tried pushing the crest, then the corners.

"It's been there for over two hundred years," Dan said. "Maybe it needs a little help." He took out a pen-knife from his pocket. He fit the blade into the mortar surrounding the tile. "If I can just . . ."

"Dan! We're in a *museum*!"

"*Dur.*"

"Someone could see!"

"Well, you'd better be a lookout, then," Dan grunted as he pushed the penknife in. He could feel the tile loosening. He heard Amy's footsteps pattering away. His sister was so rule-happy. It really got in the way sometimes.

He eased the knife farther and wiggled it. He could just manage to get his fingers behind one corner. He pulled carefully. The tile fell out, right into his hand. Behind the wall there was now a narrow hole. Dan reached inside, hoping his fingers wouldn't find a scary, crawly Egyptian insect instead of a Clue.

But his fingers met something smooth and round. He pulled out a slender leather tube.

"Just what do you think you are doing?"

The bellowing voice almost made Dan drop the tube. He hid it behind his back as an Egyptian man dressed in a gray suit yelled up at him from the bottom of the stairs. He was heavyset, so he probably wasn't too thrilled about climbing up toward Dan. Still, he looked like some sort of museum official. And he was carrying one of those walkie-talkie jobs that would no doubt bring security goons in seconds.

Excellent lookout job, sis.

He heard Amy's quick steps behind him on the stairs. "Uh, w-w-w—" he heard her stammer. As usual, Amy's brain froze in the face of authority.

But Dan was used to encountering red-faced adults. It had started with his preschool teacher, Miss Woolsey, and had gone on to homeroom teachers, art instructors (love that poster paint!), principals, the Boston fire department. This guy would be cake.

Then Dan remembered he was in a foreign country. With jails. Did they throw eleven-year-olds in jail in Egypt?

The man's eyes narrowed. "What do you have there?"

"Uh, this fell off the wall." With one hand, Dan held up the tile. Behind his back, he waggled the tube.

"Those tiles are original to the house! They are fragile!"

"That's my point," Dan said reasonably. To his relief, he felt Amy grab the tube. "It fell off." He held up the tile. "You want it?"

"Young man, don't you dare—"

Dan launched the tile into the air.

He had time to admire the man's surprising grace as he leaped forward, terror on his face, to catch it. Then he scrambled up the stairs behind Amy.

"Did you see that guy?" he panted. "He could play right field for the Red Sox!"

"I wish," Amy said, "you'd stop . . . getting such a kick . . . out of stealing things!"

They heard pounding feet behind them as guards joined the chase. They made a quick right turn and raced down a narrow hallway. Dan skidded into a small room. He threw back the screen and leaped onto the balcony rail.

"It's not a long way down," he told Amy. "Besides, you should be getting good at this by now."

"I don't *want* to be good at this," Amy said, gritting her teeth as she swung one leg over the rail. "I want to be good at library research." She swung the other leg over. "Ice-skating." She lowered herself over the side, hanging on with her eyes closed. "Baking brownies . . ."

"Let go!" Dan shouted, and Amy let go. He followed.

He felt the shock of the courtyard stones shudder up his ankle bones. He hadn't expected it to hurt . . . quite so much. Amy fell over and rolled. She gave him a fearful look. He nodded to let her know he was okay.

Someone shouted overhead in Arabic. Dan didn't need a translator. Someone was definitely not happy.

"What are you doing on the ground?" Nellie asked as she strolled out from one of the rooms leading off the courtyard. "And have you seen the ladies' room?"

Without answering, Dan and Amy raced toward Nellie, scooped their arms through hers, and started to drag her to the entrance.

The guards hit the courtyard and started to run.

"Oh, no, don't tell me. Not again!" Nellie groaned.

"Yell later. Now, run!"

"Sorry! We love your beautiful country!" Nellie yelled.

They charged through the front door while the shouting echoed in the courtyard behind them. The taxi was waiting, and they jumped in.

"Where to?" the taxi driver asked, waking with a start.

"Just go, go, go!" Nellie shouted.

"Go, go, go!" the taxi driver shouted gleefully as he stomped on the gas, practically sending them through the roof. "I love Americans!"

CHAPTER 4

As soon as the taxi joined a raging river of traffic on a main street and they were sure they hadn't been followed, Nellie gave the driver the name of their hotel. Then she crashed back against the seat and sighed.

"You two owe me, big-time. I just left my soul mate waiting for me to get back from the ladies' room."

"Don't worry," Dan said. "You'll always have cardapop."

"Carda*mom*," Nellie corrected.

"We'll make it up to you," Amy said. "Anyway, we found something."

Amy held up the leather tube. She unwound the old, worn straps and popped off the top. Turning over the tube, she shook it gently. They gasped as a small fragment of rolled parchment fell out of the tube into her palm.

It was dry and crumbled at the edges. It was so fragile Amy was afraid to even breathe on it.

"I think it's an old letter," she said. "Or at least part of one." She unwrapped it slowly.

Dan groaned. "Not French again!"

et pour la plus grande gloire des descendants de Luc et mon Empereur, l'indice est maintenant en route pour le Palais du La Paris. B. D. 1821

"Translation?" Amy asked Nellie.

"'And for the greater glory of the descendants of Luke and my Emperor, the clue is now en route to the palace o . . . '" Nellie stopped, tilting her sunglasses down to read. "'. . . *du la Paris*'? Of the Paris? That isn't correct. Unless L is an initial?"

"So who could L be?" Dan wondered.

"Well, there were an awful lot of kings of France named Louis," Nellie said. "One of them lost his head, but he had a palace called Versailles."

"Anyway, some clue was shipped off to some palace by the Lucians," Amy said. "But I wonder who B.D. is." She sighed. "I was hoping it would be a message from Napoleon."

"Does this mean the clue is back in France?" Dan wondered.

Amy carefully put the paper in her waist pack. "If we just keep digging, this will make sense sooner or later."

They had been so intent on the letter that they hadn't noticed when the taxi turned off a main street and into a quieter neighborhood. Palm trees lined the boulevard. Bougainvillea bloomed in explosions of pink and purple. "Wow," Nellie said, cranking down her window and sticking her head out to sniff the air. "I smell rich people."

The taxi pulled into a long, curving drive. Amy and Nellie gasped, and Dan cried out, "Sweet!" as the hotel came into view.

It was a big white sprawling mansion of a building. Long green lawns stretched up to its front porch. A couple dressed in white terrycloth robes strolled across a side patio toward a turquoise pool. A pool boy rushed up to lead them to a cabana. Waiters glided through the chairs, balancing trays of iced drinks. Across the Nile loomed the great pyramids of Giza, appearing through the yellow air like a dream.

Nellie whistled. "A lifestyle to which I am ready to become accustomed."

"How can we afford this?" Amy asked.

"We do have the money from the Kabras," Nellie said. "Which totally belongs to us now. We earned it."

"We sure did," Amy said, remembering Ian's double-cross. Mr. McIntyre, Grace's lawyer, had told them *Trust no one* at the very beginning. She shouldn't have forgotten that for a moment. Instead, she'd looked into Ian's dark eyes and fallen for his lines. *Dumb. Really dumb, Amy.* She had no trouble with lessons at school. But when it came to real-life emotions, she'd score an F.

"Still, we could run out of cash pronto at a place like this," Nellie said. "Maybe we should try some-place else."

The taxi had already pulled up. A snappily dressed bellman ran to open the door. Another raced to collect their bags. Before they could protest, they were ushered out of the taxi, and the driver was heading back down the drive.

The bellman hung their shabby backpacks and battered bags on the rolling cart as though they were fine luggage. Nobody gave their T-shirts and crumpled jeans a second look.

"Welcome to the Hotel Excelsior," the first bellman said. "Follow me, please."

They trailed behind him as Nellie smoothed her hair, Amy tucked in her shirt, and Dan tried to grab his backpack from the cart.

There were more wide smiles from the clerks at the front desk. One slim, handsome gentleman waved them over. "Please, welcome to the Hotel Excelsior. May I inquire the name of your party?"

"Uh . . . ," Nellie said.

"Oh . . . ," Dan said.

"Oh?"

"Oh," Dan said firmly.

"I'm sorry, the reservation is not showing up," the man said, consulting the computer. "I can recommend several other hotels. . . . Excuse me," he said as the phone rang. His posture grew even more erect as he listened for a moment. He looked at them, then turned a shoulder and spoke quietly into the receiver. "Ah, certainly, sir. I'll arrange that right away for you." He hung up and turned back to the computer screen. "*Oh.* Of course. The Oh reservation. We've reserved the Aswan Suite, as usual."

"Suite?" Amy blurted.

"At the usual family discount, of course," he added. He pushed the register toward Nellie. "If you would just sign."

Amy peeked at the price. To her surprise, it wasn't much more than the price of the fleabag hotel in Paris. Nellie signed the register and the desk clerk handed over three card keys.

He reached over to ding the bell.

"The bellman will show you upstairs."

"Family discount?" Amy hissed.

"We *are* family," Dan pointed out. "Technically."

"Your crazy Cahill family really spread out over the globe," Nellie said, admiring the huge vases full of flowering branches. "So technically, you have family everywhere. Just think of all the five-star hotels we can crash, if only we can get hold of frequent-traveler cards. . . ."

"Shhhh," Amy warned as they stepped into the elevator. The bellman swiped their key card through a slot, then pushed thirteen.

When the elevator doors opened, the bellman led them into the hallway. There was only one door.

"Where are the rest of the rooms?" Nellie asked.

"The suite occupies the entire floor," the bellman said. "I think you will like it." He swiped the key card through the slot. "You must swipe this in the elevator, too. Only you have access to this floor."

He pushed open the door, and they gasped. Floor-to-ceiling windows gave a view of the Nile and the pyramids of Giza beyond. They stood in a living room with an armchair, two sofas, an eating area, and a desk. As the bellman pushed open the door to the bedroom, Dan practically danced behind him.

"We've got three bathrooms!" he yodeled.

Nellie fished in her bag for a tip and the smiling bellman left, closing the door softly. As soon as he was gone, Amy flopped down on the armchair, Nellie kicked off her shoes, and Dan jumped on a sofa. They all shouted a rousing chorus of "Woo-hoo!"

Nellie let Saladin out of his cat carrier. "Welcome to the lush life, Sally," she said, giving him a kiss on the top of his sleek head. Saladin roamed around, sniffing, jumped up on the desk, tightroped over the back of a sofa, picked the biggest, fluffiest pillow, curled up, and blinked at them as if to say, *I could get used to this.*

Dan bounded off the sofa and prowled around, calling out bulletins to Amy and Nellie. "The desk is full of stationery! Here's a guidebook! Hey, there's an umbrella in the closet!" He wandered back into the bedroom and disappeared into the closet, coming out in a terrycloth robe that was so long it trailed after him on the floor. He opened a bedside drawer. "A Bible!" He shut the drawer and searched under the pillows.

Nellie and Amy followed Dan into the bedroom.

"What are you looking for?" Amy asked. "The tooth fairy?"

"Chocolate. Don't they leave chocolate under your pillow in these fancy hotels?"

Nellie giggled. "Not under. On top of your pillow, after they turn down your bed for the night."

He disappeared into a bathroom. "You should see all the shampoo!" He stuck his head out. "I know how much girls loooove shampoo." He batted his eyelashes at them. Amy threw a pillow at him.

Dan dodged it and bounded back into the living room. "Stand back, Jack. I just found the minibar!" he crowed.

Nellie stretched. "Well, I'm going to get in that bathtub, pour in about a gallon of bubble bath, and not get out until the food comes."

"What food?"

"The food you are about to order from room service," Nellie said. "Don't let Dan raid the minibar, we'll be broke in no time." Nellie reached into the closet for a robe and settled her earbuds in her ears. "Go wild with the menu, I'm starving," she said in a too-loud voice as music no doubt blasted in her ears from her iPod. She waggled her fingers in a wave and closed the bathroom door. Amy heard the taps go on full blast.

She walked into the living room. Dan was chewing on a candy bar while he stood facing the only closed door in the suite. He'd checked out all the closets already.

"Dan, Nellie said not to raid the minibar. That stuff is so expen—" Amy suddenly noticed that Dan was standing stock-still, staring across the room. He wasn't even chewing.

"What is it, dweeb? It's a door. D-O-O-R."

"Didn't the bellman say that there's one suite to each floor?" Dan said. "Okay, this place is palatial, but it doesn't take up the whole floor. We're in the east wing of the hotel. There were seven windows on this side, and we only have four."

Amy didn't bother to ask how Dan figured that out. Her brainiac brother had a computer for a brain.

So she didn't say anything as he walked toward the door, looking ridiculous in the oversize robe. He knelt down in front of it. It had an ornamental brass plate with an old-fashioned keyhole.

"Look at the keyhole. Does it look familiar?" Dan asked her.

"No," Amy said. She knelt down to look carefully at the hole. It took her a long moment, and then she said,

"It's the Ekaterina symbol. The weird dragonlike thing with the wings."

"Why is there a keyhole, when the rest of the joint uses cards? Must be some funky key that fits in there," Dan said. He looked around. "But where is it?"

"Do you think it's here? In the room?"

Dan suddenly sprang up. "Hey, Amy, remember all that boring stuff you read to me on the plane? What's the annual rainfall in Cairo?"

"An inch," Amy said. "And most of it falls between December and March."

"So why," Dan said, bolting to the closet, "is there an umbrella in the closet?" He reached in and took it out.

"I thought the handle was some sort of Egyptian design," he said, showing it to Amy. "But look . . ." He unscrewed the handle. It came off in his hand. Amy looked at the carvings on the handle. They matched the brass plate on the door. And the very end of the handle was configured like the lock.

Dan slipped out of the robe. He took the handle and fitted it into the keyhole. It slid in easily. He looked at Amy. She nodded.

He turned the knob, and the door opened.

Slowly, they walked in.

Plexiglass vitrines marched down a long, wide gallery. A series of archways connected more galleries, one after another. They saw glimpses of complicated machinery and blueprints. Framed drawings, photographs, maps, portraits, and texts lined the walls. As they crossed the threshold, lights in the ceiling blazed to life. The objects in the vitrines began to revolve. Three-dimensional holograms suddenly appeared and began to spin.

In one of the vitrines, a foil-wrapped article rotated.

"It's Alistair's microwave burrito!" Dan exclaimed. "This must be the Ekat stronghold!"

There was a soft but final thud as the door swung shut behind them. Amy sprang forward. "It's locked," she said. "But at least we have the key."

Dan looked down at his empty hands. "We do?"

CHAPTER 5

"Don't say it," Dan said. "I know, it's my fault. But this place is so yikes-worthy, I forgot about the key."

"How are we going to get out of here?"

"We'll figure it out. C'mon, let's explore."

"I don't know about this," Amy said. "What if it's booby-trapped?"

"We would have tripped it already," Dan pointed out.

Amy lowered her voice to a whisper. "Why isn't anyone here? The other strongholds were full of people."

"Because we got lucky. Come *on*. Don't be a weenie." Dan bounded forward. He couldn't resist the array of genius and ingenuity before him. Holograms shimmered, LEDs flickered. Over in a corner, a machine began to clatter, spitting out ticker tape, just like in an old movie. Blueprints of inventions projected down one wall. He charged down the gallery, calling back, "Oh, man. Thomas Edison was a Cahill! How cool is that? The lightbulb!"

Amy walked more slowly through the exhibits. While Dan circled Robert Fulton's design for a steamboat, she stared at a schematic of a submarine weapons-delivery system.

Dan let out a whoop. "The cotton gin! Eli Whitney was an Ekat. Genius!"

Ahead, Amy saw a black curtain. It seemed to suck all the energy in the room.

"Amy! We invented the bicycle!"

Slowly, she walked toward it. As she grew closer, she realized that it wasn't a curtain but a wall of shadow that was somehow created by a machine aiming light — or was it the absence of light? How was that possible? — toward a corner of the room.

"The sewing machine. Elias Howe, you rock!"

Hesitantly, she moved through the shadow. Ahead of her was a white screen. As soon as she approached, it was activated.

It took her almost a full minute to understand. At first, it was just blueprints flashing on the screen. Then numbers. She heard Dan crowing something about the internal combustion engine.

"Way to go, Marie Curie! Radioactivity!"

A slide show began, black-and-white photographs. She pressed her hands to her mouth.

Dan was right outside the shadow. "These inventions are so radical. We changed history!"

"Not *we*," Amy whispered.

Another stream of images began.

"Not *we*, Dan!" she suddenly shouted.

Dan walked through the shadow curtain. "What's

this?" he asked, studying the schematic and then peering at an old black-and-white photograph. There were more photographs to come in the slide show. Amy yanked Dan back into the brightly lit gallery.

"Hey!" Dan protested. "What are you doing? I want to see!"

"No," Amy said fiercely. "You don't. You don't want to see how *we* figured out a poison gas delivery system to kill millions."

The color drained from Dan's face.

"How *we* figured out how to split the atom and make a bomb that could annihilate a whole *city*!"

Heat made Dan's face turn red. Except for the small scar under his eye, which stayed white. It was how he looked when he was really upset. She should stop. But she didn't. Couldn't.

"Chemical warfare, Dan? Does that rock?" Amy didn't know why she was so angry at her brother. "Is genocide *way cool*?"

Amy backed away, her hands shaking. For the first time since he was a tiny kid, she had set out to make her brother cry. Which was funny, because she was the one who wanted to wail. She wanted to stamp her feet. She wanted to scream. But her eyes were dry.

"What if we're Ekats?" she whispered. "What if all that evil is part of us? Embedded in our DNA?"

Seeing the fear on her face, Dan suddenly felt afraid, too.

"Every branch had bad people in it," he said. "And

there are plenty of good Ekats, too. I mean, where would we be without Edison? In the dark, that's where. Anyway, we don't know what branch we're in. We only know we're Cahills. If I had to choose a branch based on the bad guys, I wouldn't want to be part of any of them."

Amy slumped to the floor and leaned her head against the wall. "What are we doing here?" she asked. "The more we find out, the more I have to wonder. Why would Grace *want* us to know that we were connected to so much evil?"

"I was just babbling before," Dan said. "Saying that we were responsible for that" — he jerked his head toward the black curtain — "is like saying I invented the cotton gin."

Amy gave a wan smile. "Good point. But Grace . . . she always protected us. She *loved* us, Danny. Or, at least . . . I thought so."

Dan was too stunned to even complain that she called him "Danny." That nickname had been off-limits since he was six. "You *thought* so? What do you mean?"

"Ever since we started this, we've wondered why Grace didn't help us," Amy said. "She didn't leave us a private message. She didn't leave us anything. She just lumped us in with all the rest of the Cahills."

"Like we weren't special to her," Dan said. He expected Amy to leap to Grace's defense like she always did. It annoyed him, but he depended on it, too.

Instead, she nodded. "So did we really know her at all?" Amy asked. "Think about it. There was this whole huge thing in her life, and we didn't know. Being a Cahill was so much a part of her. How *could* we have known her, really known her, if we didn't know that?" Amy swallowed. "It just makes me feel so . . ."

"Dumb?" Dan asked. "Hey, speak for yourself."

Amy didn't even get irritated. "Mr. McIntyre told us to *trust no one.* What if that includes . . . Grace?"

Amy closed her eyes. She hated saying these things. She hated *thinking* them. But she couldn't stop now. She kept trusting people who weren't worth it, and how dumb was that? Ian had played her for a sucker, and she sure had cooperated. If she was going to win this contest, she had to wise up.

"Those field trips she took us on — to museums and university libraries? She was showing me how real research was done. So that if I had to go into a place like that, I wouldn't be intimidated. What did she do after we went to the aquarium, Dan?"

"Made me repeat the names of every fish I saw," Dan said. "Plus their Latin names. I thought it was a game."

"She was training your photographic memory," Amy said. "All this time, she was *preparing* us." She waved a hand at the gallery. "For this! And why would she want us to know it? Already we've lied and cheated and stolen to get here. We've basically turned into criminals."

"I know," Dan said. "Isn't it cool?"

His voice was unsteady and he didn't meet Amy's

eyes. She knew her little brother was trying to distract her. He was afraid of what she was going to say. But she had to say it.

"What else will we do before it's over?" she asked. "Why would Grace want us to be exposed to this?" Her voice dropped to a whisper. *"Was she evil, too?"*

"Don't say that!" Dan yelled. He'd had enough of this new Amy. He wanted to shake her until the old one came back.

He could hardly remember his parents. Grace was all he had when it came to memories of feeling safe. Amy couldn't take that away from him. "Just shut up!" he told her fiercely.

He never told his sister to shut up. He could call her a dweeb or a loser or a pain, but he never told her to shut up. They weren't allowed to say those words to each other. It had been a rule their parents had, and even if he couldn't remember their saying it, Amy could.

But he wanted her to shut up. If he could have without looking like a baby, he'd put his hands over his ears. He could see by her face that she knew she'd gone too far.

But his sister had suddenly turned into a district attorney. "Why hasn't she helped us? *Why?* Think about it. We were just lucky that Nellie could come with us. Did Grace expect us to travel around the world by ourselves? Put us in horrible danger? If she loved us, wouldn't she have wanted to *protect* us? And what about the branches of the family? She must have known which one we belong to. Everyone else knows their branch. Irina. The Horrible Holt family knows that they belong to the Tomas. Even Natalie and . . ." Amy gulped. *And he who shall not be named.* ". . . her brother are Lucians. We're just . . . us."

"Stop it," Dan said. His voice shook. It was okay for him to wonder why Grace hadn't left them some kind of message. He'd been angry at his grandmother, too. But for Amy to say that Grace had been some kind of monster *grooming* them for this . . . that scared him.

It couldn't be true. Something inside him would break into pieces if it was. Sometimes he had felt left out when Grace was still alive. Amy had been more like Grace, interested in history and museums. But now it was like she was speaking every dark thought he ever had since Grace's funeral. That wasn't what Amy was supposed to do. She was supposed to *defend* their grandmother. If Amy didn't believe in Grace anymore, what did they have left . . . of anything?

He turned around, his eyes burning. He walked away.

Amy stayed on the floor. She touched her jade necklace, the one she never took off that had belonged to Grace. She felt a sick sensation inside. Something hollow was there that hadn't been before. It was the absence of something she'd depended on — Grace's love.

She's gone, Amy thought. *She's not with me anymore.*

Her head in her hands, she heard Dan's footsteps echo as he walked down the gallery, trying to put distance between them. The noise stopped. A long silence made her lift her head. Dan had walked all the way down to the third gallery. He stood in front of a vitrine, unmoving. Something about the tension in his shoulders made her instantly alert.

"What is it?" she called. He didn't answer.

She rose and walked toward him. He stood in front of three vitrines lined up in a row. Each held an identical statue of the lion-headed goddess Sakhet. The statues were only about eight inches high and appeared to be made of solid gold. Only their eyes were different. One glittered with green stones, one with red, one with blue. Each statue floated and revolved in a pool of white light.

"These must be what we're looking for," Amy whispered. She forgot the argument for now. The statues looked as coldly beautiful as jewels. "The Ekats already found them."

Dan spied a computer monitor built into one of the vitrines. He placed a finger on a touch-sensitive panel.

A hologram appeared. It was a diagram of the Sakhet. It revolved to show a cross section. On the computer screen they read:

FIRST SAKHET DISCOVERED BY NAPOLEON'S EXPEDITION
AT QUEEN'S PYRAMID AT GIZA. BELIEVED TO HAVE BEEN
LEFT BY KATHERINE. SENT TO LOUVRE AND RECOVERED.
DRAWING DISCOVERED HIDDEN INSIDE.

A drawing appeared on the screen.

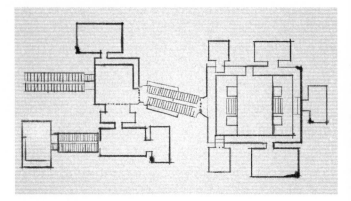

They crossed to the next vitrine, the one with the
green-eyed Sakhet. Dan touched the screen.

SECOND SAKHET FOUND BY EKAT HOWARD CARTER, 1916,
IN HATSHEPSUT'S TOMB, THEBES. EARLY INVESTIGATION
YIELDED NOTHING. STATUE HAS NOW BEEN INVESTIGATED BY
ADVANCED NDT (NONDESTRUCTIVE TECHNIQUES) INCLUDING
DIGITAL RADIOGRAPHY AND 3-D COMPUTED TOMOGRAPHY.
YIELD: STATUE IS SOLID, NO SECRET COMPARTMENT.

They crossed to the next Sakhet. Again, Dan touched
the screen.

PURCHASED BY BAE OH, 1965
SECRET COMPARTMENT DISCOVERED BY ALISTAIR OH.

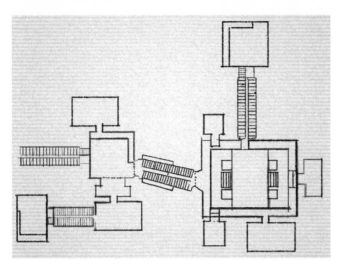

Amy returned to the second Sakhet, the one found by Howard Carter. She knew Carter was a famous archaeologist. Later, in 1922, he would go on to find King Tutankhamen's tomb.

"It says here that they studied the maps for years," Dan said. "The two maps are similar, but they have differences. No one has been able to figure it out. They think they're maps of tombs. But they don't match with any that have been discovered."

"But isn't it strange that this one doesn't have a secret compartment?" Amy asked. "Maybe Howard Carter found the wrong Sakhet. There could be another one out there."

They were so intent on studying the statues that they hadn't heard the *tap-tap* of a cane. "That is exactly right, young lady," Bae Oh said. "That's what I believe. And I believe my nephew might have it."

CHAPTER 6

Where did he come from? Dan wondered. He didn't see a door anywhere. It was like he'd just appeared out of nowhere. Creepy.

"I had the pleasure of hearing that you made a reservation in my name. I thought it might be my nephew. What a pity not to see him. I was looking forward to it." Bae smiled, but it was more like he'd bared his teeth at a dentist. "Not that it isn't delightful to see you two."

Dan didn't believe him for a minute. He thought about the locked exit door. If they had to run, where would they go? He saw Amy's glance dart beyond Bae. She was looking for a way to escape, too.

Bae's weird grin grew wider, as if he'd smelled their fear. "Do you like the stronghold of the Ekaterinas?" he asked, waving his jeweled cane. "I must confess I'm proud of it. I designed it myself."

"It's not exactly standing room only," Dan said.

Bae's grin vanished. "Even Ekats can be jealous of genius. They don't realize this has nothing to do with my own glory—I designed it for *all* Ekats. Nevertheless, am I wrong to point out that it was *I* who had the foresight to buy this hotel? It was *I* who had the vision? Cairo always had an Ekat stronghold, but it was nothing like this. A shabby house found for us by Howard Carter back in 1915, when he was searching for the second Sakhet. During the Second World War we had to hide the objects here and there, and I saw the wisdom of building a better stronghold. No one else understood the great need. It took me years. And as technology advances, I make improvements. This is as good as a museum, don't you think? Better. Such a fitting tribute to the many geniuses of the descendants of Katherine."

"Including your nephew," Amy said.

"Bah." Bae's thin mouth curled in distaste.

"I thought your name was Bae, not Bah," Dan said. "My bad!"

Bae turned his dark gaze on Dan. Dan felt a chill shudder through him. It was like having a close-up view of a shark's eyes. Right before he opened his jaws and cut you in two.

"I have heard that you are something of a wise guy," Bae said to him. "I'm sure it will get you far in life." He returned his attention to Amy. "Alistair has been a grave disappointment to me. Such a brilliant mind and such a silly man."

"Th-then why are you so interested in meeting up with him again?" Amy asked. She might be cornered, she might be scared, but she wasn't going to let this evil guy push them around.

"I am his uncle. I promised my dear departed brother I would watch out for him. When Alistair was younger, he had such promise. He was the one to discover how to open the third Sakhet. Then he goes off to become an inventor, and what does he invent? A tasteless, indigestible piece of frozen cardboard masquerading as food!"

"I heard he made a couple of cool million on that piece of cardboard," Dan said.

Bae leaned on his cane. "You must understand something. Money is not a sign of achievement. Not to the Ekats. That's why we're superior to the others. What do we value? Not power, like the Lucians, or physical strength, like the Tomas. Not even the cleverness of the Janus. No. It is something greater. Ingenuity. Inspiration. And channeling it to usefulness." He waved his stick. "You see what we have done!"

"We just saw some pretty horrifying examples of what Ekat ingenuity came up with," Amy said, gesturing back toward the black shadow-curtain.

"I thought you were smarter than that, young lady. That remark was not worthy of you."

"Why is that?" Amy challenged. "Am I supposed to be impressed with concentration camps and atomic bombs?"

Bae thumped his stick. "That is an *emotional* reaction! Ekats are not evil. They are not good. They *invent*. They *challenge*. They *lead*. Some lives lost? Those are petty concerns. What is important is the *discovery*. The *invention*. Do you understand?"

"Yeah, we get it," Dan said. "Here's the four-one-one—you are one creepy dude."

Bae Oh moved closer to them, and they backed up a step. "You are Cahills, too. You know that what makes us extraordinary can sometimes make us dangerous. Your ancestors are proof of that. It is your job to learn from their mistakes as well as their triumphs. Isn't that true?"

Amy didn't want to listen to him. But at last he'd made sense.

He took another step toward them, holding out one arm in a genial way. They backed up again. No way did Dan want to get close to this evil, ancient dude.

"Come," he said, in a tone he probably thought was warm and fuzzy. Instead, it was a total creep-out. "We are all one family. We should be allies. You've come far on the search for the thirty-nine clues, but we all need help. How about a simple exchange of information? I will tell you what I know of the great Sakhet mystery. You will tell me the whereabouts of my nephew. I know he is fond of you."

"You first," Dan said.

Bae inclined his head. "Gladly. I will show you trust, and you will do the same, I am sure." He pointed with his cane to the first Sakhet. "Here is what we Ekats know for certain. Our glorious ancestor Katherine, the queen of ingenuity, left Europe for Egypt. Can you imagine what kind of courage it took for a woman to travel alone in the early part of the sixteenth century? We know she came to Cairo and purchased three small statues of Sakhet. One had ruby eyes, one lapis, one emerald. She then disguised herself as a man and left Cairo. We know she met up with a family of tomb robbers and hired them to take her on a trip up the Nile. She hid each Sakhet, and each one hid a secret."

Bae stared at the statue. "She's beautiful, isn't she? It's no accident that Katherine chose a goddess. She believed she was never given her due as a woman. And she wasn't." He sighed. "We don't know how the other branches found out about Katherine's clue, but we know they have been searching for centuries. That horrid little Lucian, Napoleon, instructed his scholars to keep their eyes peeled for any statue of Sakhet. Some think he decided to invade the country in order to obtain it. Napoleon wasn't known for his intellect." Bae sniffed. "He had another Lucian on the expedition who did the real work. Bernardino Drovetti. He was the one who identified the Sakhet. It was in Napoleon's private collection. The Ekats made numerous attempts to steal it. Finally, Drovetti thought he could keep it safe if he shipped it off in a collection he donated to the Louvre Museum."

Amy was afraid to look at Dan. Bernardino Drovetti—could he be the "B.D." who had written the letter they'd found at Sennari House?

The clue is now en route to the palace of L in Paris . . .

"Luckily, one of our Ekats was an archaeologist hired by the Louvre. He pronounced the statue a fake and was able to get it from the museum. He smuggled it back to us for study. Ha! Right under Drovetti's nose! We found the first piece of the puzzle."

But maybe there was another Sakhet, Amy thought. *One you didn't know about. Drovetti sent it to a palace.*

Bae took a few steps toward the second Sakhet. Amy and Dan were forced to move, too, or they'd be standing close to him. "The search for the Sakhets went on. The word got out, and many Cahills came to Egypt in hopes of finding one. The great explorer Richard Francis Burton, Winston Churchill, Flinders Petrie, Mark Twain . . . none of them were Ekats. We prefer to work behind the scenes."

"Mark Twain?" Dan asked.

"Janus," Bae sniffed. "The descendants of Jane are such show-offs. It wasn't until Howard Carter made it his business to search that we found the second. Tomb after tomb, excavation after excavation. He was in competition with Flinders Petrie."

"The other great archaeologist," Amy said. "Lucian?" she guessed.

Bae nodded. "Naturally, the Ekat won. Carter found it. Here, this one, with the emerald eyes. There was just one problem. The statue is solid. We cannot find a way in. It is identical to the others, but there is no secret catch. We know this for certain. So what is the answer?

Is there another Sakhet? There must be. I myself, since I was a young man, have searched and searched. I haunted shops in Cairo, I searched through every auction catalog, I visited every black-market dealer. And then one day I found the third." Bai gazed at the statue reverently. "Blue-eyed and full of treasure."

Bae slumped over his cane, suddenly looking old and defeated. "We still were not able to break the code. We've failed at such a crucial point. We've run computer modeling and written programs to solve the mystery. There are hundreds of tombs out there that haven't been discovered yet. Any one of them could be the one. It could be that we misinterpreted Katherine's hint. Or perhaps she had a fourth Sakhet as a backup. It's impossible to say."

He took a faltering step toward them, pleading in his eyes. "I am head of the Ekats," he said in a hoarse voice. He seemed out of breath. "Alistair is my successor. If he has a Sakhet, they will welcome and honor him. I can retire a happy man. But we've had our differences. He's too proud to let me help him. But I must. For his sake, and the sake of the Ekaterinas. Do you understand?" Bae's face softened. He stepped toward them again. "I do this for him. Tell me where I can find my nephew."

Dan looked at Amy. Was she actually *buying* this? Her eyes looked soft. He tugged at her elbow, making her back up. He was suddenly wary of being within striking distance of that cane.

"Sorry to tell you this," Dan said. "But Alistair is dead."

Bae looked hard at Dan. Dan stared back at him, never dropping his gaze.

"What a pity," Bae finally said, "that you lied."

The weakness was suddenly gone. Bae moved astonishingly fast. He flipped his cane around and aimed it at the far corner of the ceiling. From one of the faceted jewels, a laser shot out. They heard a soft whisper.

A vitrine the size of a small room slammed down from above. They realized too late that Bae had maneuvered them into a specific spot. They were trapped inside four walls of unbreakable plastic with no door.

"Until you choose to tell the truth, there will you stay," Bae said. "An exhibit of fools for the descendants of Katherine to enjoy!"

CHAPTER 7

Irina Spasky was furious at herself. She'd throw herself into a gulag if she could. She deserved icy weather, thin blankets, one rotten turnip for supper. How could she let two amateurs, two *children,* give her the slip?

And if she had to eat another falafel, she'd gag. You couldn't find a plain boiled potato anywhere in this crazy country.

Enough with foreign food. Enough with the tourist disguise. Disgustedly, she peeled off the I WANT MY MUMMY T-shirt. Underneath it she wore a plain black T-shirt from the Gap. A little secret known only to her — she did love that American Gap. T-shirts in every color! She sat in a chair in her cheap hotel room and looked down at the crazy traffic. She pressed a finger against her eye, which had started to twitch. She had to think.

She had almost had those kids, *twice,* and she'd lost them! Was she slipping?

She wanted back on her home ground. She had done some operations in Cairo when she was with the KGB. She didn't operate well here. The people were too friendly. If you asked someone for directions, they'd walk with you and take you there. And it was so hot. Soon the snows would be covering the steppes in Russia, and here it was well over ninety degrees. She turned the ceiling fan to the highest setting.

She had another pair of brats on her hands — Ian and Natalie Kabra. They were supposed to be working together, and those two know-it-alls kept trying to double-cross her. Now they were in Kyrgyzstan, not answering their cell phones. She'd finally had to resort to calling their parents. And she never liked to talk to the Kabras. They had a history together, and she trusted them even less than their kids.

Those two. Geniuses, but stupid.

Just like their parents.

Their parents . . . Irina shook her head, trying to rid herself of the memory.

She never thought about things she couldn't change. Things in the past. Except suddenly, here in Cairo, she found herself thinking about Grace Cahill.

It had been years ago that the Lucians had called a top-level meeting to discuss the Grace Cahill problem. They knew Grace had collected many Clues. She seemed to have a genius for it. Even the Lucians had to admit that. She had to be stopped.

It was Irina who had come up with the idea of the alliance. Just a ruse, of course. But it could be a way to get close to Grace, to learn something. Irina had offered herself to be the go-between. The cheese in the mousetrap.

She had met with Grace. Alone, and face-to-face. The conversation had been short. It was clear that Grace hadn't believed Irina for a moment.

You're trying to play me for a fool, but it is you, Irina, who is the fool, Grace had said. *You offer an alliance as a ruse instead of a reality. It is the curse of the Lucians to think they can do everything alone.*

Irina had walked away furious. Nobody called her a fool. Nobody.

Talks resumed on the Grace Cahill problem. Plans discussed and discarded. Overtures to others. Shaky alliances agreed to in order to attack a shared problem. All to the good. Except . . . the plan had been agreed on, and everything had gone wrong. Horribly wrong. Grace's daughter and son-in-law had lost their lives in that fire.

She would never forget the day of the funeral. Irina knew it was not her place to go, yet she couldn't stay away. It hadn't been to gloat, no matter what Grace thought. Grace's face had been so white and still. The loss of her beloved daughter, her treasured son-in-law, the tragedy of her orphaned grandchildren—she had seemed years older. She moved like an old woman and her eyes held limitless grief. Her hands shook as she tossed roses onto the caskets as they were lowered into the earth.

Irina had wanted to say, *I too have known such grief.* But she didn't.

She wanted to say, *I walked the streets of Moscow like a ghost. I lost my soul, I lost my heart.* She wanted to say, *They think that grief is noisy, Grace. They think you'll cry and wail. But I know that grief is as silent as snow.*

I too have lost a child.

She said none of these things. Her memories were her own. She had sealed them off. The only relic of that time was an eye that twitched when she was under emotional stress.

That day she had blamed Grace for forcing her to recall her memories. She had been brusque and chilly. She had said to Grace, "Fate has no scruples. These things happen."

These things happen, she had said to a mother who had just lost a child. She'd heard her own words echo and been shocked at their coldness. She'd wanted to turn back. She'd wanted to show compassion, to be a person with blood in her veins.

But she hadn't. Instead, she had felt Grace's contempt run over her, like wave after wave from the cold Bering Strait. Then, in a flash, contempt turned to suspicion.

Irina had not been able to meet Grace's eyes.

So, to say the least, she had been surprised to be invited to Grace's funeral. It was only when she knew the other Cahills were invited that she decided to go.

All of them in one room. All those ancient hatreds. And Grace as the puppet master.

Had Grace set a trap that she couldn't see? Who was the cheese? Who was the mouse?

What is your plan, Grace? You always had a plan.

Those grandchildren—why did Grace include them? They couldn't possibly beat the rest of the Cahills for the Clues. They were years behind in knowledge and training. Too late to catch up. They had been lucky so far. Only that. Two children without anyone to help them, running on fear and loss . . .

Fear.

Loss.

The things I've known. The things I've seen . . .

She felt her eye twitching. She clapped a hand to her face, trying to halt the shivering nerve.

The past was past.

Except here she was in Egypt, and everywhere she turned, the very air seemed to whisper that the past was very much alive. . . .

CHAPTER 8

It had to happen. After all these years of hating museums, he'd turned into a permanent exhibit. Dan pressed his palms against the wall. "Help," he whispered.

"How much longer do you think he'll leave us here?" Amy asked.

"Until we crack," Dan said.

"How can we crack? We don't know anything."

"I know I'm hungry," Dan said. "If Oh offered me a pizza, I'd think of something."

"Nellie will start to wonder where we are," Amy said.

"She'll never find us."

"She'll tell the front desk. Maybe they'll call the police. . . ."

"Don't you get it? He owns the hotel. They're not going to do anything."

"He can't just leave us here." Amy's voice quavered, and she swallowed hard. She had been in worse spots, she told herself. But somehow this Plexiglas cube made her feel panicked. Like she was a thing on display, not a person. She tried to take a breath. "How much air is in this thing?"

"I don't know," Dan said. "Maybe . . . maybe we shouldn't talk."

Now she had scared her brother. Losing his breath was a real issue for him. Amy straightened her shoulders. She wasn't going to lose it. She'd freaked out in front of Dan before, and she wasn't going to do it again. Ever.

"I'm sure there's enough." *For how long?*

The thought rose and she batted it away. The panic eased a little. She could do this. She knew now that the trick to being brave was not thinking of the worst thing that could happen. It was a weird thing—if you *acted* brave, you could almost *feel* brave.

She'd just have to work at it. As hard as she could.

"Kiddos?" Nellie called from the bedroom. "There'd better be food out there waiting for me!"

No answer. "Dudes?" Nellie knotted the sash of the thick hotel robe. "Munchkins?" They hated when she called them that. But no howl of dismay came from the other room.

Nellie pushed open the door. The room was empty. A robe lay on the floor next to a broken umbrella. The kids had flown the coop.

Well. Who could blame them? They were in a five-star hotel, and they wanted to explore. Nellie flopped on a sofa and gave herself up to a luxurious perusal of the room service menu.

Twenty minutes later, she'd plowed through quite a bit of the delicious assortment of small dishes called *meze*. But even with the last bites of *sabanikhiyat,* she realized that her stomach was more full of worry than spinach.

Something was up. It had taken her way too long to realize it. Alarm bells should have been clanging *way* before this. She was getting sloppy. Blame it on hunger or jet lag, but there was no excuse. *You've got some explaining to do if you don't kick your brain into overdrive, Nellie.*

She had been schooled not to show panic, so she didn't. She sprang up and inspected the room. For the first time, she took note of the robe on the floor by the door. At first she'd assumed that it was Dan's usual sloppy habits, but when she studied it again, she realized that the way it was lying meant that someone had flung it off in a hurry. While standing facing that connecting door . . .

Nellie sprang forward. She examined every inch of the door. Then she looked at the broken umbrella on the floor. And everything suddenly made sense.

She saw them before they saw her. Her heart squeezed. Just clapping her eyes on them gave her a nice rush of relief. But how was she going to get them out of there?

She took a breath and composed herself. She had to keep them calm.

Amy heard the slap of flip-flops and whirled around. The fear in her eyes turned to relief. "Nellie!" She could hear her clearly. The cube must have been wired for sound.

Nellie took a bite of her pita. "What *is* this place?" she asked.

"Nellie? Uh, notice something?" Dan asked. "Like, *we're trapped in a cube*?"

He was trying to act casual, but she could hear his breath was short. She had tucked his inhaler in her robe pocket in case he needed it. But it would be better if he didn't.

Nellie took another bite. Even while she chewed, she assessed the situation with a cool glance. Saladin appeared and brushed against her ankles. "You two are an au pair's worst nightmare. This could be a way for me to keep tabs on you. It's, like, a method."

"NELLIE!" they shouted.

"He could be back any minute!" Dan said.

"Who?"

"Bae Oh! He's the one who put us in this thing."

"That old dude you told me about? What did he do, arm wrestle you?"

"NELLIE!"

Nellie walked around the cube. She tapped it with a fingernail. "Any suggestions?"

"Look up in that far left corner," Amy suggested. "The circuit is up there."

"He pointed a laser at it," Dan said.

Nellie slapped the pocket of her robe. "Whoa, I think I left my laser pointer back with my PowerPoint presentation."

"Nellie!"

She walked directly over to the corner and peered up. "I see it," she said. She reached into her pita, then bent down and fed it to Saladin. "He loves hummus," she said. "Who knew?"

"Well, he is an Egyptian Mau," Dan said. "Maybe this is home cooking for him."

"This is no time to feed the cat!" Amy exclaimed.

Saladin licked his cat lips and began to rub against Nellie's legs, begging for more.

Nellie scooped out another blob of hummus. She looked up at the corner again. She aimed and fired the blob up at the ceiling. One of her many skills, besides making the best grilled cheese sandwiches on the planet, was perfect aim. Saladin followed her gaze. "Go ahead, kitty. Go get it!" Nellie urged.

Saladin leaped up on a vitrine. He gathered himself to spring. He flew up to the ceiling and landed on the metal fretwork that held the lighting system. He casually stepped to the end of a beam, leaped over to the circuit, and began to lick the activator.

The cube shuddered a bit, then slowly began to rise.

"Get out of there!" Nellie roared. "Once he finishes the hummus, you're cooked! The beam will reactivate."

Amy pushed Dan through the opening and rolled out herself. She snatched her foot away just as Saladin lazily jumped to the floor and the cube slammed back into place.

"Cat tongues are awesome," Nellie said with satisfaction.

Amy stood and dusted off her knees. "How did you know where we were?"

"It took me awhile," Nellie said. "Then I saw little dude's robe on the floor. That was a major hint."

"Wait a second," Dan said furiously. "Little dude?"

"Now, ordinarily I would think that opening a door with an umbrella would be, like, odd. But I've been hanging around with you two, so I figure, why not?"

"Bae could be back at any minute," Dan said. "I think we'd better ditch this place and find another hotel."

"Bae Oh owns the hotel, remember?" Amy pointed out. "How are we going to get out of here without being spotted?"

"Simple biology," Dan said with a glance at Nellie's robe. "Protective coloration."

Bae Oh nodded politely at the man in black. "There was no need to come," he said. "The situation is under control."

"Have you located your nephew?"

"I am close to ascertaining his whereabouts," Bae said. An overnight stay in the Ekat stronghold would get him the information. The grandchildren of Grace Cahill were amateurs. They would break.

"There are too many factors out of our control," the man in black said. But Bae stopped listening. He'd heard a cat yowl. Pets were not allowed at the Hotel Excelsior.

Under the cover of his sunglasses, he could pretend to listen to his companion while searching over his shoulder. A family of tourists in white robes was heading toward the pool. They wore hats from the gift shop, a good thing. Profits from the gift shop paid for his vacation in Maui last year. They carried large canvas tote bags. Tourists always packed too much.

A room service cart rumbled by the group. *Mrrrrrreowwwwwrrrp!* It was the oddest cat sound he'd ever heard. Unless they had a bag of hamsters in there with it.

The smallest member of the group bent down and spoke into the tote bag.

For the first time, Bae noted the footwear. Black high-tops.

The Cahill grandchildren. *How did they get out?*

Even when agitated, Bae did not believe in making a fuss. He saw hotel security rounding the corner. Dressed in the same white pants and shirts as the waiters, you would never guess their true function. Unless you noticed the tightly packed muscles underneath their shirts and the earpieces in their ears.

All he had to do was lift a finger. Nod in their direction. The man in black was still talking. He hadn't noticed a thing. It wasn't in Bae's best interest to let the man in black know that the Cahill grandchildren were trying to escape from his hotel.

The security men moved toward the group swiftly but quietly. Things would have gone perfectly well if the young girl hadn't been conducting surveillance of her own. She spotted the trio of guards before they'd gone too far. With a quick word, the three turned and started to run.

There was no noise. No one yelled or screamed. The man in black kept talking. Bae watched as the group took off toward the back of the hotel. They paused only briefly to retrieve a large duffel from behind a bush.

Balancing luggage and an angry cat in a bag, they ran. The security detail was only yards behind as the fugitives rounded a corner.

Bae stifled a yawn. He didn't need to see the end of this little chase. He had the best security in Cairo. They would be caught and handled carefully so that guests wouldn't notice. They would be brought to his office. They would be held there. He was in no hurry. Let them sweat.

"I assure you, everything is under control," he told the man in black.

Skittering on the loose stones of the drive, Amy, Dan, and Nellie flew around the corner. Nellie tried to keep hold of Saladin as well as her canvas carry-on. Amy's backpack bumped against her back, and Dan's sneaker came untied. When he risked a look behind him, the guards were gaining.

"We'll never make it," he puffed.

Suddenly, a car peeled out of a parking space. It skidded to a stop in front of them, blocking their path.

A tiny white-haired woman dressed in a loose embroidered white tunic and pants leaned out the window. "How about a lift?"

They hesitated.

"Oh, fudge. First things first. Maybe I should introduce myself. I'm Hilary Vale, and I have a message for you. From Grace. Oh, what lovely robes."

Pounding footsteps behind them. "Stop right there!" one of the guards yelled.

Hilary reached behind and opened the back door. "I don't think this is a time to hesitate, ducklings. Hop in."

CHAPTER 9

Hilary Vale drove through the Cairo traffic with one foot on the gas and one hand on the horn. She accelerated, braked, wrenched the wheel to take advantage of sudden tiny spaces that she could swerve into.

"Get out of my way, you muppet!" she yelled cheerily out the window at anyone who dared to cut her off.

Dan's eyes shone. "She's awesome," he whispered to Amy.

Finally, she skidded off the main road, zoomed through a lovely section, and pulled into a driveway that wound through a garden thick with palms and flowering trees. She jerked the car to a stop in front of a gracious white house.

They got out of the car, feeling a little dizzy from the fast ride and their narrow escape. The house was cool and silent after the noise and heat of the streets. Hilary turned immediately into a small sitting room. It was furnished with rugs and deep sofas covered in chintz. A piano sat in a corner. Shaded china lamps sat on tables, and vases were heaped with masses of blooms.

Hilary opened the shutters. As the sun poured in, Amy could see that the sofa cushions were frayed, and that a table had been placed to disguise a hole in the rug. Shabby but comfortable, a place to flop and read for hours. Her shyness ebbed a little, just being in this room.

"Now, just take off your . . . uh, robes, and make yourselves comfortable," Hilary said. "I guess you forgot to pay for them, ducks. Is that why those awful beefy men were chasing you? You poor dears."

"Right," Dan said. "We didn't realize they took robe theft so seriously here."

She put her fingers lightly on Amy's chin and tilted her face to the light. "You look like Grace," she said. "Cute as a bug!"

"Hey. Check this out," Dan said.

Amy saw that Dan was looking at a silver-framed photograph on the piano. She walked over. It was a black-and-white photograph of two young women in front of the Sphinx.

She recognized Grace immediately. Her hair fell to her shoulders, wavy and dark. She wore a white dress and pumps. Her slender, tanned arm was linked with the blond, petite girl at her side.

"Grace was my best friend," Hilary Vale said. She gently picked up the photograph. "We met at boarding school in the US. I was sent there when World War Two started—my parents stayed in Cairo. Grace was my family for many years, when communication was so difficult during the war. She took me in, even though I was younger and had a funny accent. After the war, I invited her back here to stay on holiday. She loved Egypt." The sadness left her gaze suddenly as Hilary clapped her hands. "But it's time for tiffin! You children get cozy-comfy, and I'll be back."

"What's tiffin?" Dan whispered. "A cat?"

"A snack," Nellie said. "That's always good news." She put down Saladin's carrier and flopped on the flowered couch. "Did Grace ever talk about her?"

"I don't remember," Amy said. "I knew she'd been to Egypt, but she didn't talk about it much." Well, she did and she didn't. It was all so vague.

Cairo is a fascinating city.

Have you been there, Grace?

Of course, love. Many times. Oh, brrr, *look at that cold rain. What do you say we go bake some brownies to cheer ourselves up?*

Deflection and disguise. Now Amy realized how often Grace had changed the subject when asked about her travels. Distrust snaked through Amy, tipping her off balance again.

In the floor-to-ceiling bookshelves were more photographs. Amy picked up one in a silver frame. Someone had written over the image with a white pen—*Us, Luxor, 1952.* Grace was dressed in trousers that looked dusty and a pale shirt with her sleeves rolled up. She was squinting into the sun. Hilary Vale wore a flowered dress and a broad-brimmed hat. It looked as though they were standing in front of some kind of temple. Grace was jokingly making an Egyptian pose, her wrist bent and her hand flat.

Just then Hilary came into the room carrying a large tray and set it down on a round polished table by the window. Nellie quickly moved to help her place the platters of pastries and sliced fruit in the center.

"I see you're looking at those old photographs," Hilary said. "Hard to believe I was ever that young, isn't it? Grace came every year and stayed with me. For years and years."

"Every *year*?" Amy asked.

"She might have missed a few now and then. And of course near the end of her life travel became difficult. She told me about the cancer — she was very frank. But I was still so shocked when I heard. I never thought anything would defeat Grace."

Hilary gestured at the chairs, and they all took their seats. Amy ran her hands along the polished wood of the arms. Maybe Grace had sat in this chair. She wished she could feel closer to Grace, just from thinking that. But she couldn't.

Hilary poured a milky liquid out of a beautiful silver pitcher. "This is called *sahlab*," she said. "They serve it in the cafés all over Egypt. I hope you like it."

Amy took a sip of the drink to be polite. It was creamy and sweet, like nothing she'd ever tasted, but she could barely swallow. Her throat felt tight with tears that threatened to spill over if she mentioned Grace's name.

"This is amazing food," Nellie said, crumbling a cookie and feeding it to Saladin. "So, you say Grace contacted you before she died. What did she say?"

Amy threw Nellie a grateful look. Nellie had seen her shyness and had taken over for now. She could always count on Nellie. Dan was too busy scarfing down lemon cake to notice her.

Hilary smiled and rose. "Yes, let's cut to the chase, as you Americans like to say. Grace sent me a letter and asked me to pass some things along." She went to a small cabinet and opened it. She took out several items and went back to her chair, holding them in her lap. Amy felt an urge to grab them and run away to look at them in private, but she forced herself to take another sip of her drink and stay very still.

Hilary placed a book on the table. "First, this is the travel guide to Egypt that Grace used for many years. She wanted you to have it." She pushed it across the table to Amy.

It was a thick book, the cover warped and stained, the pages well thumbed.

"Of course it's outdated," Hilary said with a smile. "But things don't change much here."

Amy flipped open the book. She saw notations in the margins in Grace's loopy handwriting.

Great meal here, 1972 trip

Well, that didn't sound too helpful.

"This is her last Christmas card," Hilary said. "There's a message in it for you."

She handed the card to Amy. Dan scooted his chair closer so he could see it.

The card was from the Museum of Fine Arts in Boston. Grace had taken them there many times. It was a reproduction of an old painting, the Magi arriving with gifts to the manger.

Dearest Hilary,

A Merry Christmas and love sent to you and yours. My grandchildren, I believe, will arrive in Cairo soon. It is time for me to collect on the promise you made me long ago.

Please pass along this message to my dearest Dan and Amy –

Treasures,
Egypt is full of wonderful things.
Welcome – I hope you'll be happy there.

It's a country that still resinates with me, even in my dreams. If only I'd been <u>half</u> the grandmother I should have been, I would have taken you there myself. I only wish I could be there with you as you follow in footsteps I made long ago. Don't forget the art! You can always end with the basics. With all my love, Grace.

P.S. Mrs. Fenwick sends her best to S!

Amy and Dan looked down at the card. Grace's hand had held the pen and made those lines and loops. She had used a fountain pen, the way she always did for important notes. There was a blob on the end of the "g" in "grandmother." Even though they knew she'd been sick when she wrote it, the handwriting was strong and clear. She had known they would read this after she was dead.

Even the misspelling of *resonates* made Amy feel woozy, as though her grandmother was just in the next room, writing Christmas cards and calling out, "Bring me some eggnog, will you, sweets? I can't seem to locate my Christmas cheer!"

She had left them a message. After all these weeks of wondering, here it was. Yet, what *was* it? It was personal—she had called them her treasures all the time—and yet it was impersonal at the same time. She sounded so cheerful, urging them to see Egypt. As though nothing else was going on but *sightseeing.*

She looked over at Dan. She knew that his expression mirrored her own—bafflement and hurt. What kind of a final message was this?

Dan reached for the envelope. "The postmark is Nantucket," he said. "From last year."

Amy and Dan exchanged a glance. In that glance they left this room, this hot, strange city, and went to a place they knew well. Grace owned a small house in the town of 'Sconset on the island of Nantucket, off the coast of Massachusetts. They remembered blue skies and cottony clouds, air that tasted like salt. Grace grilling corn on the cob and making lime butter. Grace shouting, "Last one in is a boa constrictor!" and the sting of the cold, fresh ocean.

"Remember Ye Olde Fenwick?" Dan asked.

Amy smiled. Betsy Fenwick had been their neighbor. Amy no longer remembered which of them had given her that nickname. She came from "one of the oldest families on Beacon Hill" in Boston, which she managed to work into every conversation. She disapproved of Grace, who let her roses run wild and who gardened in old trousers and a Yankees cap.

Mrs. Fenwick disliked cats but saved a particular hatred for Saladin, who for some reason chose Ye Olde

Fenwick's garden for his own personal bathroom. Grace said she didn't understand the fuss—after all, wasn't she saving Betsy Fenwick money on fertilizer? But as it was with all jokes, Mrs. Fenwick didn't get it. She banned Saladin from her garden and insisted that Grace hang a bell on the cat's collar. Saladin had hated that bell. He considered it beneath him. *Am I a cat or a doorbell?* he seemed to say.

Amy's smile faded. Remembering Nantucket made her feel even more mixed up. All that time they had! Nothing to do but enjoy summer. All those long afternoons, those evenings watching the sun melt into the ocean . . . all that opportunity for Grace to turn to them and say, *By the way, you have a birthright. And a burden. I need to fill you in.*

"'End with the basics,'" Nellie read. "What does that mean?"

"Whenever she took us on a trip, Grace wouldn't let us read the guidebook first," Dan explained. "We had to look first, *then* read what someone else had said about it."

Hilary took a small box from her lap and said, "And now for my promise. This has been in a safety deposit box in Cairo for over fifty years. Grace gave me one key. She had the other. Her lawyer brought it just yesterday. A Mr. McIntyre?"

"Mr. McIntyre is here in Cairo?" Amy asked.

"Lovely man, if a bit stiff. We went to the bank together and opened up the safety deposit box. Inside

was only this box. He told me that you would be arriving in Cairo shortly and I was to open it in front of you.
Do you see the seal? I'm supposed to show you that it
is unbroken. Now. Let us proceed."

Hilary broke the seal. The lid creaked as she opened
the box. There was a small item wrapped in linen.
"May I?"

Amy and Dan nodded. Gently, Hilary picked up the
object and unwrapped it.

Emerald eyes stared at them, ancient and knowing.
It was the golden statue of Sakhet.

CHAPTER 10

Hilary sucked in her breath. "Blimey! If this is genuine, it's worth a fortune. Grace, you're a sly one."

You have no idea, Amy thought.

The only difference was that this statue sat on a beautiful gold pedestal. Amy stared at the goddess. She had been eroded by time, but she was feminine and strong.

"She rocks," Nellie said.

"If it's a fake, it's a very good fake," Hilary said. She hesitated.

"What is it?" Amy asked.

"Well. On Grace's very first trip to Cairo—the one we took together in 1949—she asked me for a favor. For a friend, she said. Did I know an expert forger, someone who could produce a most perfect fake. And, as a matter of fact, I did. Grace knew that my father—he was an antiquities dealer—had fakes made of his most valuable pieces during the war. Just in case the Germans stole them, you see. I gave her the name, and

I never heard another thing. So this . . . well, it could be a very expert fake. Someone added this cheesy pedestal later on, obviously."

"Obviously," Amy said, blushing. Oops—she'd thought it was beautiful. Clearly, she had a lot to learn about museum-quality statues.

Amy exchanged a glance with Dan. Grace had made a fake. Could it be that Grace had *stolen* the original Sakhet—the one found by Howard Carter— and replaced it with a copy? Bae had told them that the statues were hidden during the war and it took a few years to retrieve them and build a new Ekat stronghold. In the confusion, could Grace have gotten her hands on one? Could *this* be the original that Howard Carter found? No wonder that with modern analysis techniques they couldn't find a secret compartment!

She looked again at Grace's message to them.

Egypt is full of wonderful things. . . .

Amy remembered from her research that when Howard Carter found King Tutankhamen's tomb, he was the first to look in, and when he was asked what he saw, he replied, "Wonderful things." Was Grace quoting Carter to let them know that the Sakhet had once been Carter's?

There was only one way to find out. If there was a secret compartment in this Sakhet, it was the real one. Amy felt a chill travel up her spine, and she shivered. Katherine Cahill could have held this very object. Could have placed a hint inside with her own hands.

"If you need to get it authenticated, I just happen to have an expert in the house," Hilary said.

"That would be me," Theo Cotter said, walking into the room.

Amy, Dan, and Nellie looked up with guilty expressions. They knew they'd left him in the lurch at Sennari House. "You know him?" Nellie blurted.

Hilary smiled. "A bit."

Theo leaned over and kissed her. "Hello, Grandmother." He turned to Amy, Dan, and Nellie. "Ah, here are the culprits. Let me give you lot a tip. Curators can get touchy when you throw objects around a museum. I had a bit of explaining to do."

Just then Theo caught sight of the Sakhet. He gave a long, low whistle. "What's this? So you *did* find a real dealer after we got separated."

"No, Theo," Hilary said. "They came upon this piece in a different way." She spoke to the three. "I must confess something here. Theo came home and told me of his encounter in the Khan. He told me your names."

"But our hotel? How did you know where we were staying?" Amy asked.

Theo held up a scrap of paper scrawled on a boarding pass. It was a phone number written in Nellie's handwriting. They'd called the hotel reservation number right before they boarded the plane. "Call me Sherlock Holmes. Just don't make me wear that hat." He picked up the statue and ran his fingers over it. His voice was hushed. "Sakhet. The most powerful goddess of them all. Goddess of divine retribution and vengeance. Legend says that Ra once sent her against his enemies and she nearly destroyed the entire human race."

"Whoa, that's one Rambo goddess," Dan said.

Nellie looked impressed. "You sound like you know what you're talking about."

"Theo is an Egyptologist," Hilary said proudly. "He was a curator at the British Museum."

"I thought you said you were a tour guide," Nellie said.

"During holidays, while I was studying for my degree at Cambridge," Theo answered. "If you want to sell the Sakhet, I can put out some feelers, and—"

"No!" Amy and Dan cried together.

"I mean, it has sentimental value," Amy said quickly. She glanced at Dan. As usual, they were able to communicate without speaking. They both knew they needed help. They had to trust Grace's best friend. Grace had led them there for a reason.

"We think Grace left us a message inside that statue," Amy said. "We're on the trail of . . . a family heirloom, and we think maybe this is it."

"But isn't *this* the heirloom?" Hilary asked. "If Theo thinks it's real, it could be quite valuable."

"Priceless, actually," Theo said. "But of course there are always those who are willing to put a price on the priceless. Usually because they have pots of money."

Amy and Dan hesitated again.

"You mean you're after something *more* valuable?" Theo asked.

"Well," Nellie said, "value is in the eye of the beholder when it comes to family heirlooms, isn't it? My family has been passing along the most hideous vase shaped like a pineapple for *ages*."

Dan picked up the Sakhet. Amy watched her brother. Something had kicked in behind his eyes. A great Egyptologist like Howard Carter hadn't been able to discern the Sakhet's secret, but she'd still bet on her eleven-year-old mad-hot genius of a brother.

"Remember how Ye Olde Fenwick put up that fence just to keep the cat out?" he said. "Only it didn't?"

"Saladin figured out how to open the latch," Amy said. "He jumped up on the top, and with one paw pulled against the fence post, then . . ."

"At the same time, pushed his nose against the latch. Which, for some crazy reason, popped the whole thing open."

"Mrs. Fenwick never understood how he got in."

"It was that push-pull thing at the same time. Seemed to be opposite forces, but actually . . ." Dan pushed one finger against the nose of the statue and pulled at its neck.

"No!" Theo cried, horrified. "Don't—"

Theo took a step forward, as if he could stop Dan, but they all gasped when the head of the statue suddenly revolved halfway. A small opening was revealed. Dan peered inside. "I think there's something in there."

"Let me. *Please.*" Theo hurried to a desk in the corner of the room. He took out a small bag and withdrew a long pair of tweezers.

"May I?"

Reluctantly, Dan handed over the statue. Theo placed it on the table, then carefully slid the tweezers inside. His fingers moved delicately. Slowly, painstakingly, he withdrew a rolled piece of paper from inside the statue.

"Papyrus! How old?" Hilary asked, her voice quavering with excitement.

Theo frowned as he placed the papyrus on the desk. "It's not an ancient papyrus. Sixteenth century, perhaps? Not my area of expertise. It's got some kind of drawing on the back, and writing on the front."

"We've got to see the writing. How do we unroll it?" Amy asked.

"Carefully." Theo handled the pages by their edges and unrolled it. "This is mad," he muttered. "This should be going straight to a museum." But he, too, bent over the papyrus with the same eagerness to read it.

> Gizeh, Aswan, Thebes and Cairo,
> This land of queens and goddesses will guide you
> Under ancient stars step by step to mind
> As mile by mile the trail shall wind
> Two shall aid you, one of dread
> One makes green with tears long shed
> Where heart of her heart was found
> The rosy pillar riseth above the ground
> At noon, the shadow cast shall show
> Upon the long protecting arm, and lo!
> Five stones down, ten to the side
> Where my mark ere long ages shall reside!
>
> *K.C.*

"K.C.," Dan said under his breath to Amy. "Katherine Cahill!"

This was stupendous. Katherine herself had left the message. Which meant that Grace had been the only one to know about it, and now . . . they were the only ones. Amy grabbed Dan's arm.

"'Two shall aid you, one of dread,'" Dan read.

"Sakhet is sometimes called the Mistress of Dread," Theo said.

"Let's look at the drawing." Dan carefully turned over the delicate paper.

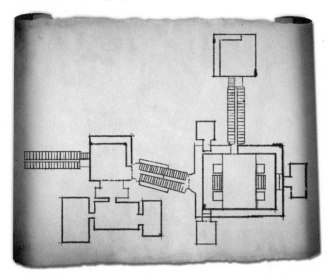

It was a drawing similar to the ones they had seen in the Ekat stronghold.

"Can you tell what it is?" Amy asked Theo.

He gave it a careful look. "I'd say it was a map of a tomb, but it would take some research to figure it out. There are hundreds of tombs all over Egypt, and more being discovered even now."

"Wait." Dan reached for two pieces of paper from the pad on the desk. Quickly, he sketched out the other two drawings they'd seen in the Ekat stronghold, remembering them exactly. He placed the two papers next to the third and looked at them all side by side.

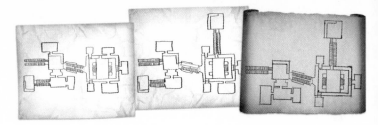

"They're all similar," Theo said. "With small differences, but . . ."

"The differences are the point," Dan said.

He took another piece of blank paper. He bent over the paper, drawing intently, every so often checking the other drawings. "You have to look at all three, then just eliminate everything except what's common to all of them." He pushed his own drawing toward Theo. "Now do you recognize it?"

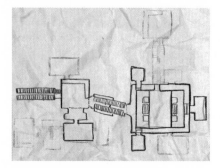

Theo looked at the map for a few long moments. Then he crossed to the bookcase and took out a book called *Valley of the Queens*.

He flipped it open to a page. "There. I thought so. That's a map of the tomb of Queen Nefertari." He looked up at them. "But why?"

CHAPTER 11

"I thought it was Nefertiti," Amy said, trying to stall.

Theo shook his head. "Different queen. Queen Nefertari, favorite wife of Ramses the Second. He ruled Egypt for sixty-six years during the Nineteenth Dynasty, New Kingdom, 1279 to 1213 BC."

Dan sighed. Everywhere they went, it seemed, he got a lecture.

"Nefertari's tomb wasn't discovered until 1904 by the Italian archaeologist Ernesto Schiaparelli. It was closed for a long time—about thirty years—because the wall paintings are so vulnerable. It was carved out of limestone and the reliefs were damaged by water, humidity, and salt. Then it underwent a massive conservation effort back in the early nineties. Now it's regarded as the most beautiful tomb in all Egypt."

"But I don't understand," Hilary said. "You can't take anything out of the tomb. Why do you have a map of it?"

"It's hard to explain," Amy said. "There might be a message there for us."

"I see," Hilary said, even though she clearly didn't. "A kind of game?"

"Exactly," Amy said. "A sort of scavenger hunt."

"Wacky family, huh?" Dan said.

"Well, you could have a problem," Theo said. "The paintings are still so fragile that they limit access to the tomb. Very difficult to get in and have a look. I might be able to blag my way in. . . ."

"Why don't you let Theo be your guide down to Luxor?" Hilary suggested. "My doctor has forbidden me to travel — he's such a fussbudget, I'm only seventy-nine — but Theo will be a perfect guide. He's led tours down to Luxor many times. He knows every inch of the valley. Let us help you, my dears. For Grace. I could do nothing for her in her final illness. Let me do this. I'll ring and make the plane reservations right now."

Dan nodded. "All right," Amy said.

Hilary looked at the Sakhet. "I have a suggestion, dears. Now that you found your note, you might want to put her back in the bank. She's too valuable to tote in your luggage. I'd be happy to do that for you."

Amy reached for the Sakhet. She wrapped the statue back in the soft linen. She zipped open her waist pack. The Sakhet fit perfectly inside. "Thanks, anyway. I'll keep her with me." Hilary was probably right, but somehow Amy couldn't let go of the statue Grace had wanted them to have, not even for a day.

There was so little she had left. The jade necklace, and now this. Grace had reached out and sent them something. She didn't understand where Grace was leading them or why, but she wasn't about to let it go.

The sun had barely risen when Hilary knocked softly at their doors. They ate a hasty breakfast and Hilary gave them another hair-raising ride to the airport. She offered to watch Saladin while they were gone.

"Don't fret a bit, ducks," she said as Saladin hissed at her. "I love felines. We'll get along just fine."

The airport terminal was hot and crowded. They stood in line, waiting for their boarding passes. The flight to Luxor was a little over an hour. They would be there mid-morning if it left on time.

Amy felt like the crowds were pressing in on her, making it hard to breathe. So many people pushing their way to ticket counters and gates. She clutched Grace's guidebook. She'd looked through it last night before going to sleep. It was clear that Grace had used the book on many trips to Egypt. Amy could tell from the different inks Grace had used. She'd dated her trips on the inside cover, from the 1960s through the 1990s. Most of the entries were about cafés she'd liked, or the names of drivers she'd used. Many of them had been crossed out. Amy wondered why Grace hadn't just bought another guidebook. Anyway, there was no message in the margin like, *Here's where you'll find Katherine's Clue!*

There had been one ink color that looked fresher. She'd looked inside the cover but it wasn't dated like the others were. Amy had thumbed through the book until the type had blurred, looking for notations in that light blue ink. She'd fallen asleep with the book next to her on the pillow.

Theo led them to their gate. They stood to the side, watching passengers disembark from a flight from Rome.

Suddenly, they heard a commotion.

"Yo, my man. In the usual, I get an escort off the plane. The fans, they have a tendency to *adore* the Wizard. They spread the love, and it can get just a little too real, you know what I'm saying?"

Dan groaned. "Oh, no."

Amy pulled him behind a pillar and gestured frantically at Nellie. Theo followed them curiously.

They peeked around the pillar. Jonah Wizard stood with his father and a tall woman in a uniform, part of airport personnel.

"Check out that mob," Jonah Wizard said.

"Those are the passengers awaiting the next flight," the woman said.

They could hear the clank of Jonah's gold chains as he turned back to the attendant. "Solid. We've got some lead time. But as soon as I step foot out there, there's going to be pandemonium a-go-go. Fo' shizzle."

"A go . . . fosh . . . Excuse me, sir?"

"I'll be calling your superior about the lack of crowd control," Mr. Wizard said. "And I can't access my BlackBerry!"

"Do you know that young gentleman?" Theo asked in a low voice.

"I wouldn't throw the term *gentleman* around," Dan said. "It might hit him and some manners might stick."

"Don't you know him?" Amy asked. "He's a huge star in the US."

At Theo's blank look, Nellie said, "You know, 'Get Your Groove Pants On'? 'Turn Back the Feet of Time'? 'You Makes My Funk Go Fresh'?"

"Are you speaking English?" Theo asked.

"We're talking street," Dan said. "Except it's Rodeo Drive in Beverly Hills."

Theo held up his hands. "Help, I need a translator!" he said.

"He's a big, fat phony," Dan said flatly. "That's all you need to know."

Amy decided to leave out the fact that Jonah was a Cahill, and a cousin. At first she'd been totally thrilled to find out that the famous hip-hop star was actually related to her. Part of the Janus branch of the Cahills, Jonah had accepted the 39 Clues challenge. Of course, it was easy for him to walk away from a million dollars. He probably spent that much a year on tips.

Jonah swept out into the waiting room, sunglasses on. He held up his hands in order to ward off requests. There weren't any.

"Send a porter for the bags. My limo will be at the curb," he told the attendant.

"I'm sorry, sir, you'll have to proceed to baggage claim."

Jonah looked startled. "I don't *do* baggage claim, mama. The bags come to *me*."

"My name is Miss Senadi. I'm sorry, sir, if there's nothing else—"

"Don't you know who I am?"

Behind Jonah's back, the attendant rolled her eyes at the other attendants at the desk. "Frankly, no."

Jonah looked stricken. He took off his sunglasses. "Dad!" he wailed.

"Don't worry now, Jonah," his father said soothingly. "Obviously, here in Egypt, they aren't aware that you're a global brand."

"You mean . . . nobody knows who I *am*?"

"Now, Jonie, just calm down, I'm sure that—"

"They don't know that I'm da *bomb*?"

An older woman swiveled. "Did someone say *bomb*?"

Miss Senadi spoke rapidly into a walkie-talkie. "Security. Security, we've got a five-one-oh."

"Oh, man," Dan said. "Did he just say the wrong thing, or what?"

"We'd better board our flight," Amy said. "I have a feeling Jonah is going to be stuck in interrogation for quite some time."

"Security, my mans!" Jonah held out his arms. "It's about time! If you can just surround me on the way to the limo—"

"I'm sorry, sir," the security man said. He took his elbow. "You'll have to come with us."

"No touching," Jonah said. "I don't accept the touching of the merchandise."

Another security guard took his other elbow, and they lifted him off his feet.

"Daddy!"

Amy and Dan giggled as the security guards force-marched Jonah and his father away.

"I haven't seen anything so funny since that TV weatherman farted in the middle of a forecast," Dan said gleefully. "I hope they keep him in detention for at least a year."

"Excuse me?" A polite young Egyptian man stood next to Dan. "For you from a friend." He handed Dan a note.

"Who was it?"

"Paid thirty-dollar baksheesh. Bye, now!" The young man ran off before they could ask anything else.

Dan unwrapped the note. It was a drawing of a long tool.

"What's this?" Dan asked. "A hoe?"

"That's not a gardening hoe," Theo said, glancing at it. "That's an ancient Egyptian embalming tool used during the mummification process. They used it to get the brains out of bodies. Up through the nostril, jiggle it about a bit until the brain liquefys and pours out the nose."

"Cool!" Dan said.

"My sentiments exactly. They didn't preserve the brain like they did the other organs, though. The lungs, stomach, and intestines were removed and each placed in a different canopic jar."

"Wow," Dan said. "I'm impressed. Way to go, ancient dudes!"

"A friend of yours sent the message?" Theo said. "Rather amusing, I suppose."

"Yeah," Amy said. "It's hysterical."

CHAPTER 12

As they wound through the streets of Luxor, Dan started to feel like Egypt was the oven and he was the turkey. He was glad when the cab drove down a small lane to a dock and he could see the green water of the Nile. He didn't feel any cooler, but it was better than looking at sand.

"Where are we staying?" Amy asked Theo as they all grabbed their bags.

Theo paid off the driver. He pointed with his chin to a small, trim white sailboat, sitting low in the water. "There."

"Whoa," Dan said. "A boat? That rocks."

"Exactly," Amy said. "And it doesn't stop." She'd never been crazy about boats. And it hadn't helped that she'd almost drowned when she'd been thrown off one into a canal in Venice.

"These boats are called *dahabiyyas*," Theo said. "Do you see the smaller sailboats out on the river? They're called *feluccas*. No trip to Egypt is complete without a Nile cruise on a felucca. My friend said we can stay for a couple of nights on his boat while he's in Cairo."

"Hey, maybe after we go see Queen Neferfarty's tomb, we can go for a swim in the river," Dan said.

"It's Nefertari, and whatever you do, don't swim in the Nile," Theo said. "There are parasites — worms — that could make you very, let's say, uncomfortable. The larvae penetrate the skin. And, of course, there's the occasional crocodile."

"Okay, you convinced me," Dan said.

"Come on, let's take our gear aboard."

The cabin was trim and spare and gleaming. There was room for two people to sleep in the bow, and a seating area made up another bed. Bookshelves lined the sides of the cabin. Theo said he'd sleep on the deck. "To watch out for crocodiles," he said with a wink.

"Now," he said, "I have to go see about those passes to the tomb. Might take a little persuasion. You'll want to take a rest later when it gets really hot, but you still have time to explore the Valley a bit. Where would you like to start?"

Amy thumbed through Grace's guidebook. On the plane she'd noted that Grace had outlined a site with light blue ink. "She said not to miss the Temple of Hatshepsut."

"Brilliant. Both sites are on the Thebes side of the river." Theo looked at Nellie. "How would you like to see a real archaeologist's office?"

"Really? I'd love it."

Dan rolled his eyes at Amy. They had never realized that their smart-mouthed au pair was so capable of being . . . a *girl*. He'd practically gotten airsick watching them share their bags of peanuts on the plane. He wished Nellie would go back to worshipping her iPod.

"Let's stroll down to the Corniche and I'll put you two in a taxi," Theo said to Amy and Dan. "Nellie and I will meet you at Hatshepsut's temple in exactly one hour. Then it's off to the tomb."

"I can't believe Theo said that it isn't hot yet," Amy said. "How much hotter can it possibly get?"

She was about to grumble more, but ahead of her, an incredible sight was rising in the wavy desert air. The Temple of Hatshepsut sat at the foot of towering cliffs. It was built in three tiers, with columns marching along the front. A series of ramps and stairs led up to it.

"Isn't it amazing?" she said.

"Which part?" Dan asked. "The sand? Or the sand?"

"Here we are, walking on ground that people walked on thousands of years ago. I was reading in the guidebook—"

Dan held up two crossed fingers. "Lecture alert."

"—that this temple was designed by the queen's architect, Senenmut, in the Eighteenth Dynasty. Later it was damaged by Ramses—"

"I guess he wasn't a fan—"

"—and it was even a Coptic monastery for awhile. They're still excavating parts of it. I think we should go right to the reliefs of the queen's journey to the Land of Punt. Look at what Grace wrote."

Don't miss these! Even back in the New Kingdom, a queen had to go Christmas shopping.

"Where's Punt?" Dan asked. "Is it next to Pass and Hike?"

"No one knows for sure. They think it's present-day Somalia. Hatshepsut led an expedition there."

They came to the wide ramp, which had shallow stairs in the center. The heat bounced off the pale stone and pounded against their bodies. The pale yellows and beiges of the sand and the cliffs turned everything into a pulsating shimmer. Amy was glad Theo had insisted they wear sunglasses and baseball caps. The glare was blinding. As they ascended, Amy felt more and more transfixed. It made her dizzy, heat and blue sky and cliff and the grandeur of the statues and the columns.

"There she is," Amy said, pointing to a statue of Hatshepsut.

"Whoa, she has a beard," Dan said. "The queen is a dude!"

"She called herself *king*," Amy explained. "So sometimes she's portrayed with a beard."

"Whatevs," Dan said. "I still think she needs a shave."

"Come on, I think the wall reliefs are on the second tier." Consulting the guidebook, Amy stopped for a moment. Dan tried to peer over her shoulder.

"I think we go right," Amy said.

"No, left."

"Right. *Then* left, then right again—"

"And turn and kick and jump. Are these directions or a cheerleading routine?" Dan tried to grab the book. "Let me see."

"No, I've got it."

"I haven't even seen it yet!"

Amy wrenched the book from Dan's grasp. "I don't want you to lose it."

"I'm going to lose it, all right," Dan muttered darkly.

Amy hurried ahead. She didn't want the book out of her sight. Grace's messages were in there, and even if she couldn't figure them out, she didn't want Dan spilling soda on the pages or forgetting the book in some café.

Dan scowled as he trudged behind her. Amy kept looking up at the massive walls and checking the guidebook, anxious to find the exact spot. Suddenly, she stopped and pointed. "There! This is right where that picture of Grace was taken." She stood where Grace had been standing and struck the same pose.

"I don't get it," Dan said. "A bazillion years ago, a queen goes to Punt. I don't see what that has to do with us. Hey, look at that."

He pointed to a short, squat figure. Amy consulted her guidebook. "That's the Queen of Punt. She gave the gift of myrrh trees to Hatshepsut."

"I don't care, she should still lay off the falafel."

"Why did Grace lead us here?" Amy wondered out loud. "What is she trying to tell us? It's so frustrating!"

"But at least she's *trying*," Dan said. "She finally left us something to go on. She left us the Saladin hint so we'd know how to open the statue. Only the two of us would know about that."

"I guess you're right." Amy looked out over the valley, then along the line of tourists heading up the sweep of the ramp. She picked out two figures straggling behind. "Look!" she cried. "It's Jonah and his father."

"Oh, no," Dan groaned. "I was hoping they'd stay locked up for at least eternity."

Suddenly, the glare made them feel exposed to every eye. Dan and Amy looked down as the tiny figures of Jonah and his father suddenly stopped. Jonah sat down, right on the ramp, as if he was too hot and tired to go another step. His father bent over, obviously trying to urge him to get up.

"Where's Theo and Nellie?" Dan wondered. "They should have been here by now."

Amy felt a shiver of alarm. "Let's go look for them."

They headed up to the next terrace. As they reached the top of the ramp, they saw Theo and Nellie standing by a column.

"We've been looking for you!" Nellie said, even though it seemed to Amy that she and Theo had been standing there, holding hands.

"I have bad news and good news," Theo said. "Bad news — Nefertari's tomb is closed."

"Bummer!" Dan said.

"The good news is that Theo is amazing," Nellie said, giving Theo a starry-eyed gaze. "You should have seen him in action. He gets to the main top guy, some big-whoop archaeologist, and he starts talking about how he's writing this book, and the guy is so impressed with how brilliant Theo is that he gives us a pass and says we can visit the tomb! Pure genius!"

"You're exaggerating. It was nothing," Theo said.

"Don't be so modest," Nellie said.

"It had nothing to do with me. It was because you were so charming."

"Um, hello? Mutual admiration society?" Dan said. "Tomb?"

"Right-o," Theo said. "We'd better go now, before he changes his mind."

"Is there a back way?" Amy asked. "I'd, um, like to see some stuff the tourists don't see."

"I always know the back way, remember?" Theo asked. "But don't forget this—when it comes to tombs, there's only one way out."

<hr />

"Okay, we have a few rules to follow," Theo said. "This tomb is in a very fragile state, so absolutely no cameras, no flashes, no flashlights. Once I open the door, the lights will come on. You'll be able to see, but it's not very bright. The frescoes must be protected at all cost. Watch your step on the stairs, and don't touch any of the walls. And when I say it's time to leave, we *go*. We have ten minutes. Agreed?"

They all nodded. Theo swung open a heavy iron door. He disappeared into the tomb and they followed down the narrow stairs. The air was cooler as they descended, and smelled of dust. Amy heard Dan cough. She hoped the close air wouldn't aggravate his asthma.

Theo spoke in a hushed tone. "The tomb was found empty. Robbers had stolen everything long ago. But this tomb has a greater treasure."

They stepped into the first room. Amy sucked in a breath. Colors jumped out at her, alive and beautiful. Reds, golds, greens, blues.

"There, that's Nefertari. Her name means The Most Beautiful."

The figure wore a transparent white gown with a wide golden collar and earrings in the shape of flower blossoms.

"She's beautiful," Nellie said. "I totally want her jewelry."

"Look up," Theo whispered.

Over their heads the ceiling was painted a deep blue. Golden stars were painted in a few swift strokes, row after row. It made Amy feel dizzy.

"The tomb is designed so that Nefertari says good-bye to life as we descend," Theo explained. He led the way down a flight of narrow stairs. "Various gods greet her and help her on her journey. The final room is the tomb room."

They walked past other wall paintings, vivid and beautiful. "That's Osiris," Theo said, pointing. "God of the underworld, husband of Isis. When we enter any tomb, we enter the world of Osiris."

They passed through into the burial chamber. "Here, Isis leads Nefertari to the underworld," Theo said. "Look how tenderly she holds her hand. And she places the ankh, the symbol of eternal life, against her mouth."

Amy had forgotten about the Clue. It was hard to focus with so much color and mystery around her. She was in the center of an ancient world, and all she could do was turn around and around to gather in as many images as she could.

"Our ten minutes are up," Theo said.

"But they can't be! We just got here!" Amy said.

"Time stops down here, doesn't it? But we have to go. Did you find what you were looking for?"

"No, but it was amazing," Amy said. How could she pick out a single hieroglyph or a drawing? Everything was ancient, existing thousands of years before Katherine Cahill was born. Katherine must have seen this tomb, must have walked through and been stunned by its beauty, just as they had. How could she have left something here that she knew would be found? She wouldn't have left an object; her guides were tomb robbers, so she knew that objects wouldn't be safe.

Amy gave a last glance behind as they climbed back up to air and sunlight. *What did you leave, Katherine?* she wondered.

As they returned to the boat, they saw the white paper fluttering from the mast. "What's that?" Amy asked warily.

"Maybe it's a takeout menu," Dan said. "Do mummies eat pizza?"

They jumped aboard and walked closer. Nellie gasped. The piece of paper had been attached to the mast with a lethal-looking knife. The blade glinted in the sun.

They stepped closer to read the message.

> Death shall come on
> swift wings to him who disturbs
> the peace of those who sleep.

"This is way too creepy," Nellie said with a shudder.

Theo extracted the knife and crumpled up the paper. "Must be the locals trying to scare us for their own amusement."

Amy didn't think so. "But what does it mean?" she asked.

"It's the pharaoh's curse," Theo explained. "A silly superstition, that's all. Anyone who violates a tomb will suffer a terrible and untimely death. It's all the stuff of horror films, really. Totally juvenile."

Juvenile? Dan looked at Amy. *Jonah,* he mouthed.

Nellie sprang to set out the lunch they'd bought on the way home. "Could we not talk about mummys' curses before we eat? Really bad for digestion."

Dan and Amy sat down on chairs out of earshot of Theo and Nellie, who chatted while they ate. "So Jonah knows we're here," Dan said.

Amy scooped up some baba ghanoush with the flat-bread called *aish merahrah.*

"You're right. It's probably him. Seems like his style."

"He'd rather follow us than figure something out himself," Dan said. "But what *is* it?"

Amy squinted at her plate. "Some kind of eggplant thing, I think."

"No, what we're *missing.* We're the thirty-nine clueless! There has to be a reason why Katherine Cahill led us to that tomb." Dan had memorized Katherine's dumb poem. Now he went over it slowly in his head.

He sat up. "Hey. Remember — *Under ancient stars step by step to mind.* We thought she meant the sky. What if she meant — "

"The golden stars on the ceiling of the tomb!" Amy cried.

"Step by step," Dan said. "We looked at everything on the walls, but did we examine the *steps?* We have to get back into that tomb!"

CHAPTER 13

Irina held on to the railing. She couldn't risk stumbling on these steep stairs. She'd seen the Cahill kids leave the tomb, and she knew something must be here. A small explosive blew the lock, and she was in. Good thing she wasn't seen. Egyptians could get so touchy about their precious sites.

Irina came to a small antechamber. Those flat Egyptian figures — all the same, they were — surrounded her, some with a bird's head, some with crowns, some holding staffs curved like snakes. She poked her head into the side room. More of the same.

But the colors . . .

She wrenched her attention back to the task. More stairs. She descended carefully, glad she was wearing her Nikes. Those Americans knew how to make athletic shoes. She'd give them that. Irina kept her brain on sneakers because she was feeling a bit dizzy. It was a trick she used while on a job if she was tired or exasperated, any time her emotions threatened to overtake her. Concentrate on the trivial.

But why was she feeling overwhelmed?

To her left, a black jackal was offering something to an Egyptian queen person. It must be Nefertari. Irina didn't know anything about Egyptian art, but somehow she knew this: The beautiful queen was being welcomed to the underworld. She would leave behind her life. Sunshine, river, palace, husband, child. All would be taken from her.

She stepped inside the burial chamber. Here the queen had been laid, between the pillars.

Those flat figures, all the same, like cartoons, with their black hair and their opaque eyes. She'd never realized before . . .

How beautiful they are!

These paintings . . . she imagined artists here, dipping their brushes into pots of gold and green and blue. They weren't just painting the story of one queen's death. They were painting every life. Every death. Every joy, every loss.

Dazzled, Irina slowly revolved, drinking it all in.

She felt something odd on her face, something so foreign she didn't recognize it at first. She felt it like a draft, a coolness in this stale air. A tear.

What was happening?

Grace, what are you doing to me?

Because she *felt* her, she felt Grace suddenly, her presence, right here. Her briskness, her intellect, her impatience . . . her *kindness.*

You were kind to me, she told Grace. *When you told me I was a fool, there was no harshness in your tone. There was kindness in your eyes.*

Who can't I forgive? You . . . or myself?

Irina stared ahead at the wall. Rebirth, she realized. This chamber wasn't about death at all. It was about rebirth.

Could that happen? After a life lived, after choice after choice after choice led you someplace small and dark . . . could you . . . *change?*

CHAPTER 14

Note to self, Dan thought. *Do not think of brain-sucking mummies while standing in ancient tomb.*

The darkness pressed around them. They had just pushed on the door of the tomb, and it had swung open. Theo must have forgotten to lock it. Somehow without his cheery presence, the tomb seemed darker. Spookier.

"D-do you think we should go down?" Amy whispered.

"That's why we're here," Dan said. He didn't move.

"This is ridiculous," Amy said, straightening her shoulders. "Come on."

She eased the door shut, but left it open a crack. Dan stayed close behind her as she went down the stairs. When they got to the antechamber, they both looked up at the ceiling. The stars looked like a field of golden flowers against the brilliant blue.

They looked back at the stairs. "Let's look at the risers," Amy said. "The stone that is behind the step.

Katherine would have left a clue there rather than on the step itself. She'd know that hundreds of years of footsteps would wear away any message."

They examined each riser, but there was nothing except ancient, worn stone.

"Next staircase," Amy said. "We'd better hurry."

They cautiously made their way down the stairs, deeper into the tomb.

"Wait!" Amy whispered. She didn't know why she whispered, but it felt wrong to shout in this place.

She bent over, squinting in the dim light. She forgot her nervousness as the discovery jolted through her. "Dan, come here! I think it's a hieroglyph. It's carved into the stone."

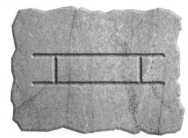

"And here," Dan said.

Down they went, collecting one hieroglyph after another.

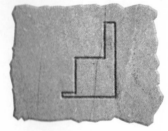

Suddenly, they heard a squealing noise, the sound of metal against metal.

There was a loud clang as the iron tomb door shut completely. The lights immediately went out.

"Amy?" Dan whispered.

"I'm right here." Amy only knew Dan was inches away by the sound of his voice. It was so dark she couldn't see her own hand. She fought down panic.

The darkness pressed against them like a living thing.

Dan felt his breath catch. Amy grabbed his hand. Normally, Dan would have pulled his hand away and said something like "Ew," but just then his sister's fingers felt good, even if they were kind of sweaty.

"Somebody shut the door," Amy whispered.

"Thanks for the tip, Miss Obvious," Dan whispered back.

Suddenly, he heard a noise. Was it a footstep? Shuffling, as if a foot was being dragged along the dusty ground. As though wrappings were dragging behind . . .

"Did you hear that?" Amy whispered.

"No," Dan lied.

DEATH SHALL COME ON SWIFT WINGS TO HIM WHO DISTURBS THE PEACE OF THOSE WHO SLEEP.

Dan knew he was breathing dust. He could feel his lungs struggling. He heard his own wheezing in his ears.

"Dan." Amy gripped his shoulder. "There's plenty of air. Do you have your inhaler?"

His sister's calm voice steadied him. He didn't know how she could be so calm, but it helped him. He knew how she'd panicked when she'd almost been buried alive. The Amester was getting braver all the time. He reached into the pocket of his shorts and brought out his inhaler.

Better.

The noise came again, terrifying in its soft menace. He didn't even bother saying he didn't hear it. He imagined a mummy, black holes for eyes, trailing linen. His brains had already been sucked out, and he was just a dead thing . . . reaching . . .

Slow down, he told his heartbeat. *If this was a video game, you'd think it was way cool.*

Another shuffling noise, closer still.

But it's not a game!

Whoever it was—person or *thing*—it was hunting them.

"We've got to hide," Amy whispered. "The burial chamber."

He didn't, didn't, didn't want to go back to the burial chamber. The thought of it froze his blood. But he followed Amy into the place the mummy had lain thousands of years ago.

Even in the enveloping dark, Irina was completely oriented. She heard Dan and Amy inching their way toward her. Her vision was like a cat's. She could find her way out of a cave miles underground if she had to. As a matter of fact, she already had, thanks to that nasty little job in Marrakech back in the nineties.

The acoustics in the tomb magnified every sound. They were coming right toward her.

This was her chance. They were hers at last. The question was, what to do, exactly. The children needed to be slowed down, they needed to be stopped. Frightened so badly that they would go back to that Boston Beantown where they belonged.

So, her poison nails—always an option. Or would a little explosive be better? Nothing too nasty, just enough to start a small cave-in. If she could get past them—and she could—she could place the device at the entrance, and *ka-blooey*. They would be stuck in the burial chamber for a good while, she imagined. Long enough to decide that the 39 Clues was a game for adults, not children.

Irina moved forward silently. Amy took a hesitant step into the chamber. The children were holding hands. *Awww.* What adorable, sniveling cowards!

The tomb had gotten to her. She'd been thinking crazy thoughts. *Blin!* As her grandmother used to say, she'd almost blown her own roof. Crazy thoughts, that she'd been on a wrong path, that there was another way to go.

There was only one way to go, and that was over everyone else.

They were close. She could smell their fear. She smiled as she moved closer. Just another millimeter or two . . . Her foot hit something.

"Did you hear that?" Amy squeaked.

Irina was so close she could reach out and touch her. She had only to extend one finger . . . and scratch.

Her eye twitched. She bent down and touched what she'd hit with the toe of her Nike. Her fingers closed around a small book. She put it in her pocket.

"Someone's here with us," Dan whispered.

Yes, I am here, little comrade. Irina could make out the gleam of the back of Dan's neck. So vulnerable. So close.

But wait. Better they should be conscious when the explosion occurred. What was the good of scaring them if they were unconscious? Terror was best experienced when one was wide-awake.

Reluctantly, Irina drifted past the children like a ghost. Up the stairs toward the door. The side chamber was to her left now. In her other pocket was the explosive.

Irina stopped. She set the timer. She held the explosive in her hand, ready to place it.

She remembered the wall paintings. The queen. The other goddess leading her by the hand. The greens, the golds, the blues. Three thousand years this tomb had survived. *It should rest in peace.*

What? How did that thought enter her brain?

She was a Cahill. A *Lucian.* Superior in intellect and cunning. She should do anything to get what she wanted. . . .

Except destroy what millennia of sand and water and thieves did not.

Irina turned off the timer.

That's when she heard the footsteps. There was someone else here.

Irina was scared of nothing in life. Except . . . maybe clowns.

She went toward the noise.

CHAPTER 15

The door clanged open. Lights went on.

"Dan? Amy? Kiddos?"

"It's Nellie!" Amy cried. "We're here!"

Nellie rushed down the second set of stairs into the burial chamber. She threw herself at them and gave them a fierce hug.

"Will you just *stop* doing this?" she demanded. "My nerves are shot! You could have been down here for, like, eternity!"

Suddenly, Theo came rushing down toward them. "Amy? Dan? Nellie!" Theo grabbed Nellie by the elbows. "Are you okay?"

"I'm fine," Nellie said.

"Amy and I are fine, thanks," Dan said.

"I was looking everywhere for you!" Theo said frantically to Nellie. "Are you certain you're all right?"

"Perfectly okay," Dan said. "We were just shut up in a tomb. No problem."

"What do you mean, Theo?" Nellie asked. "I woke up and saw Amy and Dan were gone. I knew they would head back here. Basically, I just pick the thing that would freak me the most, and they do it."

Theo wiped at the sweat on his forehead. "I got a text message on my phone that you were in trouble. I've been looking everywhere."

"Did you see anyone when you entered the tomb?" Amy asked Nellie.

Nellie shook her head. "I just rushed down the stairs when I heard you calling."

"We heard someone," Dan said. "A sort of shuffling noise."

Theo tried not to smile. "A mummy?"

"We didn't imagine it," Dan said, annoyed. "Whoever it was could have hidden in one of the side chambers, then gone out after Nellie came down to the burial chamber."

"Oh, no! Grace's guidebook!" Amy said. "I must have dropped it."

They searched over the entire tomb but didn't find it.

"Are you sure you had it?" Theo asked.

"Of course she's sure," Dan said. "She never lets it out of her sight. You see?" He looked around the tomb. "Someone else *was* here."

"And they took Grace's book," Amy said.

Amy and Dan were silent as they sat in the cabin of the boat after dinner. Theo had suggested going to

Luxor for dessert — he knew a "super" rooftop restaurant with a view of the river and the Temple of Luxor. But they couldn't think about dessert or great touristy views.

Misery hung over Amy like a cloud. Dan knew just how she felt. The book was gone. It was the same way he'd felt after he lost the photograph of his parents back in the train tunnel in Paris. It was like he'd lost a piece of them. Now they'd lost a piece of Grace. A *crucial* piece.

They kept losing piece after piece of their old lives. Falling down, falling away. Until you felt like you were on a world without gravity, and soon you'd have nothing to hold on to. Tonight, the motion of the boat made Dan feel almost dizzy.

It was time to work, not think. Thinking about stuff too much didn't get you anywhere, no matter what his sister thought.

Dan pushed a piece of paper toward Amy. "Here." He'd written out the hieroglyphs they'd found on the stairs of Nefertari's tomb.

Amy didn't bother asking if he was sure he remembered them right. She sprang up and went over to the crammed bookshelves. She slid out a heavy book. "I saw this before. It's a hieroglyphic dictionary."

They flipped through the book. It took them awhile to find the explanations for the hieroglyphs. Dan copied them down.

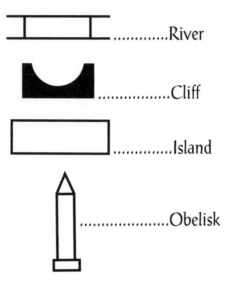

............River

............Cliff

............Island

............Obelisk

"River, cliff, island, obelisk," Dan said, pointing to each. "These are easy. But we can't find this last one."

"Okay, here we are in Luxor," Amy said. "There's a river. There are cliffs. Islands in the river. Obelisks. But Katherine can't just be listing random things."

"*If* Katherine made those glyphs," Dan said. "We don't know that for sure. She wouldn't know how to decode hieroglyphs in the sixteenth century. Hieroglyphs weren't translated until a couple of centuries later, when they found the Rosetta Stone."

"These are pretty simple, though," Amy said. "They're pictograms—they mean what they are. She would have figured them out. We could, even without the dictionary. Except for this last one."

"Things just aren't adding up," Dan said. "Maybe there *is* a fourth Sakhet. Remember that note we found from that guy Drovetti? He said the clue had been shipped to the palace of L."

"Louis the Fourteenth, maybe," Amy said. "Versailles is right outside Paris."

"Maybe we shouldn't be here at all," Dan said. "Some Lucian shipped the most important hint to Paris. This feels like it could be a dead end."

Amy's gaze wandered to the porthole. "Dan? Did you notice that the lights of town are . . . kinda far away?"

Dan stood up. "Our line came loose! We're going toward the middle of the river!"

"Excellent work, homies!" Jonah Wizard's head appeared at the top of the steps leading to the deck. "Good lead. Paris is my city! They love me in Paris!"

Amy and Dan charged toward the stairs. Jonah stepped back and let them come up on deck. They were in the middle of the river. The lights of Luxor seemed far away.

Mr. Wizard was at the helm. Jonah collapsed in a chair with a laugh, pointing at them. "You should see your faces!" he said. "Hysterical. Anyway, what can I say? If only you agreed to be my homies when I offered you the deal. Yo, Dad, book us two first-class tickets to Paris. Love that Hall of Mirrors at Versailles. So much of *moi* to see!"

"I can't get service out here," Mr. Wizard said, his thumbs trying to work his BlackBerry.

"You know what?" Jonah threw his legs over the arm of the deck chair, one sneakered foot swinging. "You both look beat. Maybe you need a vacation. Say, on a nice tropical island?"

Mr. Wizard brought the boat around. He crossed to the small gangplank on the side.

"Oh, c'mon," Dan said. "You've got to be kidding. You're going to make us walk the plank?"

Jonah chortled. "Tru dat, me hearties. I always wanted to be a pirate!"

"I'd suggest you go now," Mr. Wizard said. "We've got a plane to catch."

The gangplank thudded down on the sand of the small island. It was uninhabited. All Amy and Dan could see were thick trees and undergrowth. Amy was glad she had the Sakhet in her waist pack.

"We'll get you for this!" Dan said to Jonah.

"Yeah, what*ever*."

"And those stupid warnings didn't scare us a bit."

"What warnings?" Jonah asked. "Just walk the walk, Peter Pan. You first, Tinker Bell," he said to Amy.

Dan followed Amy down the plank.

Mr. Wizard hauled it up after they were on the island. The boat began to glide away.

"Have a slammin' time!" Jonah called out. "I'll be betting that someone will come by . . . sooner or later. Oh, but there's just one thing."

His voice sailed over open water. "Watch out for the crocodiles!"

CHAPTER 16

Amy decided she was never watching Animal Planet again. Once you'd *lived* Animal Planet, it lost its charm.

She edged away from the bank of the river. Behind her, the trees and foliage looked thick and impenetrable. Without the sun, the river had taken on a dark and oily look.

"Crocodiles have the strongest bite of any animal on earth," Dan said. "Five thousand pounds per square inch. That's, like, twelve times stronger than a great white shark. They move fast, even on land. But the best way to run away from them is straight ahead, not zigzaggy. Just run really fast."

"Dan! Zip it," Amy said.

"They hunt at night. They wait in ambush for their prey."

"This isn't helping."

"They drag you underneath the water and roll around and around with you and drown you before they chomp you. If you're lucky. You've got to get your hands around their jaws and hold them closed—"

"Dan, get lost!"

"I *am* lost!"

There was a short silence. Across the dark river, the lights of Luxor glittered. Behind them on the west bank of the river, the ancient kings and queens slept in the limestone cliffs, the mummies still undiscovered, the hills cradling their spirits. The sky overhead was thick with more stars than Amy had ever seen. It would have been beautiful if only Amy could stop worrying about getting clamped in crocodile jaws.

"I'm just trying to be helpful," Dan said.

"If we can attract a boat's attention, someone will see us," Amy said. She could see the individual lights on the ends of boats—feluccas, Theo had called them—out on the river. "How do you say *yoo-hoo* in Arabic?"

"I believe that *yoo-hoo* could be part of a universal language," Dan said. "Like *ow*. Or—you're stepping on my foot."

"That's universal?"

"No, you're stepping on my foot. Ow."

Amy moved.

"Yoo-hoo!" Her voice sounded thin. It was swallowed up by the darkness. She tried to remember if crocodiles hunted by noise. She decided not to ask Dan.

"YOO-HOO!" she shouted. The tiny boat lights stayed on their courses, tacking lazily back and forth. "Well, Nellie and Theo will come looking for us," she said.

"How will they look for us?" Dan asked. "Jonah stole the boat!"

"They'll hire a boat, and—"

"Shhh," Dan stopped her.

"Just because I told you to be quiet before—"

"Shhh! Listen."

Amy didn't hear anything. Then she heard a soft splash.

She froze. "Do you see anything?" she whispered.

"I thought I saw . . . two eyes," Dan whispered. "Out there . . . by those reeds. Crocodiles stay submerged until they attack. . . ."

Amy looked. She didn't see anything by the reeds. What she did see was a giant log floating close to the riverbank. Then she saw that the log had two eyes and a snout. The crocodile turned and began to glide toward the beach.

"D-d-d-d . . ."

"What?"

"C-c-croc . . ."

The crocodile lumbered onto the beach, and Amy forgot how to move. It looked like a walking dinosaur. Something primitive and evil and hungry for flesh. Every impulse had been driven from her brain except for terror. The crocodile opened its mouth. Amy felt mesmerized by what looked like hundreds of sharp, pointed teeth.

Crocodiles have the strongest bite of any animal on earth. . . .

"Run!" Dan hissed. He yanked at her arm.

Amy wheeled, stumbled, and took off, running across the beach toward the center of the island. The sand sucked at her shoes. It was like running in a nightmare.

Amy looked back. The crocodile was following them!

"Don't zigzag!" Dan shouted.

But she wasn't zigzagging. She was stumbling. Her legs were shaking so badly that she couldn't run.

They crashed into the underbrush, following a narrow path that snaked through the trees. Amy's T-shirt snagged on a branch but she ripped it free and kept running, jumping over roots and ducking under branches.

Over the sound of their gasping, they heard the actual *thump* of the crocodile hitting the path. The *swish* as its gigantic tail hit the greenery.

It was so dark under the trees that it was like running underneath a black hood. Amy's heart banged against her chest. She could already feel the hot breath of the beast. Any moment it would snatch her from behind and whirl her in the air as its jaws cut her in two.

The path suddenly ended, spilling them out on a beach. Moonlight silvered the sand. It was as if someone had turned on the lights.

"Where to now?" Amy asked, whipping her head around.

Down by the water, a shadow slipped away from a palm tree. A man stood, dressed in the white *galabia* that many Egyptian men wore.

"Help us!" Amy screamed.

"Amy . . ." Dan stopped short. "He's got a knife."

Moonlight glinted on the blade the man held at his side.

Amy turned around. Behind her on the path she saw the green eyes of the crocodile coming toward them. Faster. "I don't care," Amy said. "Come on!"

They ran down the beach toward the man with the knife.

Better that than a crocodile's jaws.

The man sheathed the knife as they approached him. The crocodile was running across the beach now. The man suddenly backed away, then scrambled toward a small felucca they hadn't noticed before.

"No, wait! Please!" Amy cried.

He jumped in gracefully and began to paddle. Amy sobbed out loud. Terror squeezed her heart. There was no hope left. No place left to run.

But the man was paddling *toward* them, not away. He was shouting something in Arabic.

They ran to him, faster than they'd ever run in their lives. They waded through the water, feeling like their legs were lead. The crocodile was gaining the edge of the water. If it made it in the water, they were dead. Amy knew that clearly. She could see by Dan's terrified face that he knew it, too.

The man reached out. He grabbed the edge of Dan's T-shirt with one hand, Amy's with the other. Amy felt like a fish as he hauled them up and over the side.

They lay in the boat, gasping. The sail furled as it caught a breeze. They all heard a *plop* as the crocodile entered the water. The man didn't speak. His mouth was a grim line as he reached for the rudder.

He tacked away, and the boat glided over the water, straight out toward the middle of the river. They caught a current and whirled away. They all held their breath, waiting for any movement near the boat.

Suddenly, the man smiled. He nodded at them. "Okay," he said. "Okay."

Amy's entire body was trembling. She looked at Dan. That had been way too close.

She pushed off the deck to sit up straight. Her hand landed in something wet and sticky. She brought it up to see.

Blood.

They were out in the middle of the Nile with a stranger with a very big knife and blood on the deck of his boat.

"We . . . we come in p-peace," Amy said.

The man leaned forward. His gaze was dark and blank. He reached out a strong hand and pointed at Dan. Amy threw herself over her brother to protect him. "No!" she screamed.

"Yes!" the man shouted. "Red Sock!"

"R-red . . . *what*?"

He pointed at Dan's T-shirt. "Bos-ton. 2004 World Series champs!" the man said. "Fenway Park!" He pointed to his own chest. "Game Two!"

Dan sat up, blinking as the man's words registered. "You were there? Awesome!"

"Curt Schilling!"

"Manny Ramirez!" Dan beamed and turned to Amy. "Baseball. Another universal language."

"What about that knife?" Amy hissed.

Dan began to laugh. It had finally happened. Her brother had lost it.

"Can't you smell it?" he said. "He's a fisherman. Look!"

Yes. Now she could smell it. Right next to her was a bucket of fish. He'd been cleaning them when they'd first spotted him.

"Luxor?" the man said. Now Amy could read the friendliness in his smile. She nodded.

The river was a dark, inky blue. Amy caught her breath as her heartbeat slowed. She tilted her head back. She picked out the Big Dipper in the cluster of stars. A sense of comfort trickled through her. From here she could see the moonlight on sand on the Thebes side of the river. It looked like a snowfield extending to the cliffs. As they sailed, the lights of the great Temple of Luxor twinkled.

"Amazing," she said.

"Amazing," the fisherman said.

Apparently, *amazing* was part of the universal language, too.

The fisherman left them on the dock close by the Luxor temple. With a huge grin and a friendly wave, he called, "Bye-bye, Bostons! See you later, alligators!" and sailed off.

"'We come in peace'?" Dan mimicked her. "Did you think he was an Egyptian or a Martian?"

Amy couldn't help giggling. "How did I know he was a Sox fan?"

"Where to now?" Dan asked.

"Theo and Nellie must have gotten back by now," Amy said. "Maybe they're waiting at the dock. We'll have to explain why there's no boat."

But when they got to the dock, the boat was there. Nellie and Theo sat on the deck, drinking tea. "Did you go for a walk?" Nellie asked.

Dan looked at Amy. Amy looked at Dan. Should they mention Jonah Wizard, the boatnapping, the crocodile, the big knife? The Red Sox–loving fisherman?

"Yeah," Dan said. "We went for a walk."

They left Theo and Nellie on the deck, drinking chai and watching the night sky, and went below.

"At least Jonah returned the boat," Amy said.

"At least he's on his way to Paris," Dan said. "The question is, should we be going, too?"

"I've been thinking about that. When we were in Paris, I read about the history of the Louvre Museum. It was once a *palace.* So when Drovetti wrote *palais de L,* he probably meant Palais de Louvre. Remember, Bae told us that Drovetti sent the Sakhet to the Louvre, and an Ekat managed to get it back. I bet there isn't a fourth Sakhet. After all, the three maps added up to Nefertari's tomb. Now we just have to use the hieroglyphs to figure out where to go next."

Dan frowned. "Katherine isn't helping much. And neither is Grace!"

"Well, Katherine mentions Aswan in the poem. Giza, Aswan, Thebes, and Cairo, remember? We started in Cairo. Napoleon found the first Sakhet in a pyramid in Giza. The second was found by Howard Carter in Hatshepsut's tomb in Thebes. Aswan is the only city left. I bet that's where the final clue is."

"But we don't know that for sure," Dan argued. "Bae found the third Sakhet in Cairo, but that was hundreds of years after Katherine left it somewhere. It could have been stolen and sold and sold again. It could have come from Aswan."

"Maybe," Amy agreed reluctantly. "Remember what Bae said about Katherine, that she felt underestimated because she was a woman? Haven't you noticed that Katherine has been leading us through all the *female* pharaohs, queens, and goddesses of ancient Egypt? Sakhet, Hatshepsut, Nefertari. Even the Giza clue was found in the queen's pyramid."

"That reminds me." Dan looked at the hieroglyphs again. "When Theo was giving us the tour, and that part where Isis is holding Nefertari's hand? The glyph over Isis was the same as this."

"I bet this means *Isis.*"

"Another female goddess!" Amy flipped through her book. "Ancient Egyptians believed that when Isis heard her husband, Osiris, was dead, her tears made the Nile overflow—turning the land fertile for cultivation." She looked up, her eyes alight. "*'One makes green with tears long shed'!*"

"What about *'where heart of her heart was found'*?" Dan asked.

Amy read on, her heartbeat quickening. "Osiris was dismembered by Seth. Isis found his heart on the island of Philae. That's where her temple is."

Dan put his finger on each hieroglyph. "Island. Isis. Obelisk.

"Where is Philae?" Dan asked.

"Aswan!" Amy exclaimed. "It all adds up." She closed the book with a thud. "The thing is," she added, "I don't remember if Grace wrote anything about Aswan. I wish we hadn't lost her guidebook!"

"*We?*" Dan asked.

"Okay, *me*," Amy said, flushing angrily. "If you want to blame me, go ahead."

"Well, maybe if you'd let me look at the book, we'd have an idea of what to do next," Dan said.

"That's not fair," Amy said. "You don't like research like I do."

"I can *read*," Dan said bitterly. "And unlike you, I can *remember*, too. You barely even let me look at it."

"You always say research is boring," Amy countered. "How was I to know you wanted to read a guidebook for the first time in your life?"

"It wasn't just a guidebook. It was *Grace's* guidebook!" Dan's voice rose. "You want to keep everything that Grace left for yourself. You've got the necklace and now the Sakhet . . . you won't let go of that, either. You even want to keep her *memory* to yourself!"

"That's not true," Amy protested. "And it's not fair, either!"

"Well, she's not just *your* grandmother, you know!" Dan said. His face was bright red. "You want her all to yourself!"

"Don't be ridiculous!" Amy yelled. She felt her face grow hot. "That's the dumbest thing I've ever heard!"

"*You* get to decide if she was good or not. *You* get to decide if she loved us or not. If you're going to tell me that my grandmother didn't love me at all, that she was some evil mastermind, then you'd better back it up with *facts*," Dan told her furiously. "You're so spooked you'll make a mistake again that you're doing a complete one eighty. Everybody isn't bad just because *Ian Kabra* is!"

Amy gasped. She'd never seen Dan act like this before. He called her names and fought with her, but never like this. He was never deliberately mean. He looked almost triumphant now, like he'd scored a hit.

Just like she'd felt in the Ekat stronghold when she'd made him cry.

What was happening to them? Was this what the chase for the Clues was doing to them? Betrayals and secrets were the new normal. It was warping them. Turning them against each other.

They were both acting like people she didn't recognize. People she didn't like.

They were acting, Amy realized, like *Cahills.*

CHAPTER 17

It was only nine in the morning, and the temperature in Aswan was well over ninety. In the airport, Amy felt sweat snake down her back, and she shrugged off her backpack and looped it over a shoulder. With every step, it bumped into her waist pack. She wasn't about to complain. If she did, Dan would just throw her a look of disgust and call her a wimp, and she wouldn't be responsible for her actions.

Then again, he probably wouldn't call her names. They weren't talking to each other.

Slam, slam, went her backpack against her waist pack. She trudged after the others. Nellie was first, heading toward the taxi stand. Theo had called Hilary for help, and she'd recommended the Old Cataract Hotel, "where Grace *always* stayed in Aswan, ducks . . . *darling* Saladin, do get your claws out of my arm, *thank* you. . . ."

Dan was after her, putting as much distance between himself and Amy as possible. Theo walked in front of Amy, digging for the sunglasses in his shirt pocket.

Crowds of tourists waiting for luggage milled about, and a tour guide called out, "This way, people!" as another large clump of tourists moved toward a row of buses.

Theo dropped his sunglasses and leaned over to pick them up. Amy felt someone bump into her from behind as she stopped short. She felt the chafing from the waist pack, and she reached down to move it slightly. To her surprise, she brushed a hand. "Hey!"

She felt her waist pack being tugged. The crowd pressed in on her. She couldn't turn, and she couldn't move forward. Amy started to panic. "Help!" she cried, but nobody heard her. Theo didn't turn. He was waving at Nellie. She felt as though she were being squeezed by a roomful of writhing snakes. She couldn't get her breath. It was so hot, and the moving bodies around her trapped her. She couldn't break free. "H-h-help!" Her voice was so puny, barely a squeak.

Ahead, she saw Dan turn. His eyes met her panicked ones. He knew immediately she was in trouble. He started to force his way back to her.

"Dan!"

She tried to move toward him and almost fell.

"Dan, help! My waist pack!"

Suddenly, his arm popped through the crowd and he yanked on her wrist. He pulled her as hard as he could, knocking a woman out of their way. Amy felt the pressure on her waist pack ease.

She twisted around and scanned the crowd. Instead of writhing snakes, she saw sweaty tourists anxious for ground transportation. Out of the corner of her eye, she saw someone move, but it was only an older couple, a fat man in a straw hat and his wife looking down and searching through her bulging tote bag. Amy saw the light glint on her silver snake ring.

"Hurry, you two!" Theo stood at the cab, the door open.

Amy tumbled into the backseat next to Dan.

"Hey, someone tried to saw this off from behind," Dan said.

Amy unbuckled the waist pack with shaking fingers. She saw the mark of a knife trying to slice through the canvas. At the sight of the fresh cut, a chill went down her back. "That was close."

"You've got to watch your belongings in crowds," Theo said. "I'm glad you reacted so quickly, Amy."

"It was Dan, actually," Amy said.

"Yeah, I managed to do *something* right," Dan said.

Theo looked out the window. "Why don't we drop our bags at the hotel and catch a boat over to Agilika Island right away?"

"Wait," Dan said. "I thought Philae was the name of the island. That's where the guidebook said the temple was."

"Philae is the name of the *site,* but Agilika is the island," Theo said. "Philae Island has been completely underwater since the 1960s."

"What?" Amy blurted. The Clue was under*water*?

"That's when the High Dam was built. Even before that, after the building of the first dam back in 1902, the island was submerged during certain parts of the year. People would actually look down at it through the water."

"So what happened to the buildings on the island?" Amy asked.

"They were saved and moved to Agilika," Theo explained. "The island was landscaped to look exactly like Philae. It's as close as you can get to an authentic experience. The only thing that's changed is the island itself. You'll see the Temple of Isis just as it existed on Philae."

"Do you mean that the original island of Philae still exists, it's just under the Nile?" Dan asked.

Theo nodded. "Under the lake that was created by the dam. But there's nothing to see on it now."

Theo and Nellie began to talk, and Amy spoke in a low tone to Dan. Since he'd practically saved her life, it was hard to stay as mad at him.

"We still have a chance," she whispered. "The poem said the rosy pillar would cast a shadow at noon. Since the buildings are positioned exactly the same, the same shadow will fall on the same place on the 'long protecting arm' — whatever that is. If we're lucky, Katherine's clue will still be there."

"Either that, or we need to stop at Snorkels-R-Us," Dan said.

The taxi drew up in front of the Old Cataract Hotel, a beautiful spot right on the Nile. Theo offered to take care of storing their bags and "distribute a little baksheesh." When he headed back to the cab, a bellman ran up and handed him a small slip of paper. Theo read it and frowned, then slipped it into his shirt pocket.

"What was that?" Amy asked as he slid into the front seat.

"Nothing. Just . . . a welcome greeting from the front desk."

Dan reached over the seat and grabbed it out of Theo's pocket. He scanned it quickly. "Some welcome."

He showed it to Amy and Nellie. An Egyptian drawing of Osiris, god of the underworld, was at the top. Underneath was written:

> Your arrogance will
> lead to your demise!

"I didn't want you to see another one of these silly notes," Theo said.

Dan crumpled it up. "It doesn't matter." But it did. He'd thought Jonah had sent the notes. But Jonah was supposed to be headed to Paris.

"Here are the docks," Theo said. "Let's hustle — there's a ferry leaving."

They ran for the boat and made it with seconds to spare. The ferryboat chugged away from the dock. Here in Aswan, the Nile seemed even more beautiful. The color was closer to emerald, and it was full of white sails. Large cruise ships docked nearby, tourists leaning over their railings, holding cameras and pointing. Two herons stepped delicately through the reeds, reminding Amy of the paintings she'd seen in Nefertari's tomb. Ancient and new collided in one of those startling moments she was beginning to recognize as part of Egypt.

"We're going to land at the southern tip, but it's not far to the temple," Theo told them. "Do you know the story of Isis?"

"She was married to this dude Osiris, and he croaked," Dan said. "So she freaked and was all *wah!* and went and cried herself a river."

"Amazing! That's just what it says on the hieroglyphs," Theo said.

The boat docked, and they followed Theo to Isis's Temple. It was a huge complex, tall and grand, with reliefs cut into the stone. They walked down the grand colonnade with its row of columns.

Dan looked around. "Where's the obelisk? Isn't there one here?"

"There was," Theo said. "Two of them, actually, erected by Ptolemy VIII, cut in pink granite. They were damaged—one fell over—and were removed in the nineteenth century—well, stolen, or bought, depending on how you want to look at it—by an Englishman. They're in his garden in Dorset, England."

Amy was crestfallen. The obelisks—the *rosy pillars*—were gone. There was nothing to cast a shadow now. How could they find the Clue?

Theo went on with his tour. "On the old island, the Nile would flood once a year," he said. "They built walls to protect the temples. That's one reason why the temple is so remarkably well preserved."

"But there're no walls here," Amy said.

"They didn't need to relocate them." Theo shrugged. "Because of the dam, the Nile doesn't flood anymore."

Theo moved off with Nellie. Amy slumped down on a step. "What are we going to do now?" she asked. "The obelisk is gone."

Dan sat down next to her. "So are the walls—don't you think they're the 'long protecting arm'?"

"Why did Grace send us here if the dam flooded the island?" Amy wondered. "She must have known that. And this place is so *huge*. I wouldn't know where to start."

"She must have left another hint," Dan said. "We just haven't found it yet."

There was a short silence. The ice had been broken, but the air was still frosty between them, despite the blazing sun.

"Dan, we just can't turn into bad Cahills," Amy said in a small voice. "All we have is each other. I can't do this without you."

"I feel the same way," Dan agreed. "You can't do it without me."

Amy laughed. If she was getting tougher, so was Dan. Maybe the changes wouldn't be so bad. If they could just manage to stay a family, the two of them, they could figure out how to be Cahills, too.

CHAPTER 18

That night, Amy couldn't sleep. Images collided in her head. Temples and tombs, crocodiles and lions. Ian Kabra's dark eyes and flashing smile. The squeeze of panic she'd felt in the airport as the crowd closed in. Her brother's narrow, intent face, the way he'd pushed through the crowd to get to her. The old couple, the woman looking down into her tote bag. Light glinting on the woman's silver ring.

Sleep was dragging her down, and right before she slipped into it, she saw Grace's face smiling at her and saying, *Trust people, but keep your money in your sock.*

Amy woke in the middle of the night. It wasn't as though she heard a noise. It was more that she had the memory of a noise. She fought her way up from the luxury of sleep.

Her hand fell alongside the bed, where she had a habit of resting it on the waist pack on the floor. There it was, the sharp angle of the base of the Sakhet, poking out. She started to settle back against her warm pillow again.

. . . but keep your money in your sock.

Amy reached down again and moved her fingers around the base to touch the Sakhet. Her fingers met empty air. There was no statue attached to the base.

Heart hammering, Amy came fully awake. She slipped out of bed and felt along the floor. Nothing. Under the bed. Empty.

The window was open. Had she left the window open? Amy ran to look out.

The moon was high and full and illuminated the lawn outside like stadium lights. It was easy to see Theo, duffel in hand, hurrying along the curving path. Amy saw car headlights flash in the parking lot beyond.

Amy didn't stop to think. She raised the window the rest of the way and slipped outside. Her bare feet hit the cool dirt. She snaked through the bushes, hit the grass, and took off.

Too late she realized that she'd need help. Theo was heading for that car. Could she take him down? She'd need to hit him right around the knees. . . .

She heard pounding footsteps behind her. Nellie was racing toward Theo, her face set with angry determination. Her legs flashed underneath the boxer shorts and oversize Pearl Jam T-shirt she wore to bed.

She slammed into Theo in a tackle that would have gotten her thrown out of the NFL. He went down with a howl of pain.

Amy sped past them and raced to the car. To her surprise, Hilary sat at the wheel, her mouth open in comical surprise at the sight of her grandson with Nellie on his chest.

"What's going on, ducks?" Hilary's face was pale, but she tried to keep her voice merry.

Amy reached over and turned off the engine, then pocketed the keys. "Why don't we find out," she suggested. She was surprised at her own coolness. If you got mad enough, you didn't have to try to be brave.

"*Mrrrp.*" Amy heard the soft noise and her heart lifted. "Saladin?" She reached into the backseat and took the cat carrier.

Taking a firm grip on Hilary's elbow, Amy marched her back to Theo and Nellie.

Theo's face was twisted in pain. "Did you have to hit me that hard?" he howled.

Nellie leaned over and hissed the words in his face. "Your arrogance just led to your demise, sucker!"

Theo sat on the floor of the hotel room while Amy lifted the Sakhet from his duffel. Hilary sat primly in a chair.

"I'm sure we can work this out," she said. "If Theo has done something wrong, I can take care of it."

"I wouldn't be so sure," Amy said.

"Could I at least have some ice for my ankle?" Theo asked plaintively.

"Sure," Nellie said. She went to the ice bucket,

picked it up, and dumped the contents on Theo's head.

"Thanks," Theo said.

"Don't mention it," Nellie said sweetly. "Snake."

"What should we do with them?" Dan asked. He'd grabbed the lamp off the table and was holding it, just in case Theo tried to get away. He'd bash him in a second if Theo gave him the chance.

But Theo didn't look like he wanted to give him the chance. He looked deflated and damp.

"Police, for sure," Nellie said.

"Stick a fork in him, he's done," Dan agreed.

"What are you talking about?" Hilary looked horrified. "Theo, what are they talking about?"

"Not police," Theo begged. "Please. Stealing the statue would be a capital crime. You don't want me to go to jail, do you? I'd be there for a thousand years!"

"Then some archaeologist can study *you*," Dan said.

"You don't understand," Theo said. "You didn't even seem to want the statue. It was just part of some silly scavenger hunt. You didn't realize what you had!"

"Theo!" Hilary cried. "When you asked me to meet you here, I never thought . . ." Her hands flew to her mouth.

"Oh, please," Nellie said. She crossed to the phone.

"Look, I'm sorry, okay?" Theo continued. "But after all, you know what Egyptologists make. You study for years and years, you go down into tombs, you pore over papyrus, and what do you get for it? A job offer as some assistant curator in a museum with a salary that won't even cover the rent."

Hilary buried her face in her hands. "Oh, Theo. If you'd just let me take him away, I promise . . . I'll make it up to you."

Amy stared at her hand. "That's a nice ring, Hilary."

"Thank you, dear."

"When did you get to Aswan?"

"Just now, ducks. Theo asked me to meet him; I had no idea why."

"No idea," Amy repeated. "That's funny, because I saw you at the airport this morning. You stood next to some old guy, hoping it would look like you were with him. *You're* the one who tried to saw off my waist pack!" She turned to Theo. "And you pretended to drop your sunglasses so she could do it!"

Hilary gave a laugh that sounded strangled. "What an imagination!"

"Oh, really, Grandmother, give it up," Theo said tiredly. "Do you really think you're fooling anybody?"

"I can if you'd cooperate!" Hilary hissed.

With a look at Hilary's twisted face, Amy's fury returned. Betrayed once again, taken for a fool. "How could you do it?" she demanded. "How could you betray Grace? She was your best friend!"

"Exactly!" Hilary cried. "And she had all the money in the world while I slipped into poverty. I wasn't in her will. Why shouldn't I get a piece of her estate?"

"You are one greedy old woman," Nellie said, shaking her head. "Bad karma."

Again, Amy thought angrily. She'd trusted someone, and it turned out to be the completely wrong thing to do. Now she didn't know whether to be angrier at Hilary or herself.

Theo sighed. "Look, I'm sorry I took your statue," he said to Amy and Dan. "But when somebody offers you a cool million, what are you going to do?"

Nellie picked up the phone.

"Wait a second," Dan said. "Who offered you a cool million?"

"Some crazy Russian lady."

Nellie put down the phone.

"Just where did you see this crazy Russian lady?" Amy asked.

Theo looked abashed. "In Nefertari's tomb. I bumped into her in the antechamber."

"You were the one making the mummy noise?" Dan demanded.

"I thought . . . if you got scared enough . . . you'd give me the Sakhet for safekeeping," Theo said.

"You're the one who sent those warning messages, too," Nellie said, her eyes narrowing to slits. "Admit it."

Theo nodded. He hung his head. "I'm sorry."

"Sorry? You lock my two kids in a tomb and you say *sorry*?" Nellie yelled. "I'll show you sorry!" She started to dial.

"Wait a second, Nellie," Amy said. "I think we can make a deal here." She turned to Theo and Hilary. "We won't turn either of you in. *If* you both do us a favor."

CHAPTER 19

The blond archaeologist, or should she say *thief*, seemed nervous. Probably because he was double-crossing a couple of kids whose only legacy from their beloved grandmother was a crazy contest they were bound to lose and a priceless statue. And thanks to him, they'd lost the statue.

Well, sore luck for them, Irina thought.

The guidebook had turned out to be a dead end. No hints, just notes in the margins, stupid things like *don't miss this!* and *good food here.* A big fat zero for any Aswan Clues. What a waste of time. She'd already thrown it away. Having Grace's thoughts, no matter how trivial, just made her eye twitch.

Irina circled back around to the café where Theo Cotter sat waiting, his fingers drumming on the small tiled table, the bag at his feet. She knew she hadn't been followed. She'd passed by the café three times to make sure.

She slid into the chair next to him. "You have the Sakhet?"

"You have the money?"

She inclined her head. "As we agreed. It will be wired to Swiss account once I authenticate the statue." She had no intention of wiring the money. She didn't need the statue, she needed what was inside it. Lucians had been searching for it over the centuries. She wasn't sure why, but once she had it, she'd know.

"First, I will examine in ladies' room."

She picked up the small bag, then moved through the tables to the restroom. She locked the door securely.

She turned over the statue in her hands. It was a Sakhet, she knew that, with a lion's head. Golden, as had been reported by the great Lucian Napoleon. The eyes were emeralds, she supposed — she didn't know anything about gems. Everything appeared to be as it should be. Irina tapped the statue gently, searching for the trick to open it. She saw a hairline crack along the lion's mane. She slid a narrow stiletto (so useful that knife had been over the years!) into the crack and the head revolved counterclockwise easily. It revealed a small compartment inside. Turning the statue over again, she shook it. A rolled piece of papyrus fell out.

Gizeh, Thebes, Rabat and Cairo,
This land of queens and goddesses will guide you
Straight to the place where camels wait
And donkeys file amid the strait
To the palace steps you'll find your way
As midnight strikes, full moon on bay
You'll find my answer on the quay!

It sounded like a load of horseradish. But the hints toward Clues never did make sense, until you got to the place where you were guided. Rabat was a city in Morocco. No doubt everything would be clear once she got there. Carefully, Irina slid the secret compartment closed. She put the paper in her pocket and the statue back into the bag.

She threaded her way back through the tables and plunked the bag back down at Cotter's feet. "I'm surprised you would try to cheat me," she said. "That is never good idea. This is fake statue."

"But I assure you, it's genuine."

"Ha! You think for me I was born last Thursday? No money for you." Irina got up and hurried away.

She wondered if the airport had direct flights to Morocco. The ancient city of Rabat was her next stop.

As she jumped into a taxi, she congratulated herself. She'd gotten over that brief moment of sentiment in Nefertari's tomb. She couldn't allow herself to be weak again.

Once she had the 39 Clues, she could maybe afford to be generous. Or maybe not generous, no need to go overboard. Maybe just a little . . . less strict. Until then, she would allow no more distractions. And she would never step foot in another tomb. Too many ghosts. Too many memories . . .

Irina's eye began to twitch.

"Aswan airport. And step on it with foot!"

CHAPTER 20

"It worked," Dan said. "That's good, right?"

"Right," Amy said. Irina had taken off for Morocco, and they'd seen Theo and Hilary board the plane to Cairo.

"Why do you look so bummed?" Nellie asked. "You should be celebrating. You had this great plan — you bought some old papyrus, and Theo copied Katherine's handwriting perfectly. We found the perfect fake statue and drilled the hole. Thanks to our collective brilliance, you just sent your worst enemy on a one-way trip to a wild goose chase. Besides, I'm the one who should be crying. My heart is broken." Nellie waved her spoon, then scooped up another spoonful of yogurt and honey. "Oh, yum."

"Your heart was broken for about five minutes," Amy said.

Nellie shrugged. "What, am I supposed to stop eating?" She pointed her spoon at Amy. "Never regret trusting someone. It proves you have a heart. But if he turns out to be a lying worm . . . I'm not going to waste my time crying. Because I am *way* too fabulous for that."

Amy knew that Nellie was telling her to get over Ian. Could she really borrow some of Nellie's confidence? She never felt *fabulous*. Some days if she was lucky, she hit the high mark of *not bad*.

"It was a brilliant plan," Dan said. "You knew Irina wouldn't fork over a million dollars."

"She doesn't have a million dollars," Amy said. "She was going to double-cross Theo. All she wanted was the lead. And she wanted it so badly she didn't stop to think that it came a little too easily."

"That's the fatal flaw of the Lucians," Dan said. "They think they're brilliant."

Nellie scooped up the rest of her yogurt and stretched. "I'm taking off for the pool. Suggestion — try to bypass the adventure highway for today?"

"I've been thinking," Dan said as Nellie took off. "I think Grace prepped us for this trip. Remember when she took us to New York for the weekend? We went to the Metropolitan Museum of Art and spent a bunch of hours in the Egyptian wing. Remember the Temple of Dendur?"

"That's right!" Amy exclaimed. "She told us all about the Aswan High Dam, and how it flooded all these monuments they had to rescue, like the Temple of Dendur. But that's all I remember. If she gave us a hint that day, it's lost."

"She bought us hot pretzels," Dan said. "That, I remember."

Memory bloomed inside Amy. One of hundreds that were buried in her head and heart about her grand-mother. Eating pretzels with mustard on the steps of the museum. It had been fall—she remembered the brilliant orange trees in Central Park. Grace had already been through one round of chemotherapy. They'd all thought she had licked her cancer, that she would be well, that she would live forever.

Well. Amy and Dan had thought that. Because Grace had wanted them to. For as long as they could.

What wonderful things we saw today, Grace had said. *But sometimes people spend too much time in the past. Nothing I saw today is as good as this pretzel!* She'd waved it in the air and taken a bite.

She hadn't meant just the pretzel. Amy knew that now. She'd meant everything at that moment. The now. The three of them together, sitting on the museum steps on a perfect fall day, eating pretzels and mustard from a sidewalk vendor.

The memory didn't just belong to her. It belonged to Dan. He remembered things like that. Random moments that seemed small but were actually huge. Often those moments passed her by because she was so busy worrying about something stupid like catching a bus. Or mustard on her new skirt.

She took the Sakhet out of her waist pack and put it on the table.

"What should we do with her?" she asked. "I don't feel safe carrying her around Aswan. It's your call." What she was really saying was, *Grace belongs to both of us.*

Dan met her eyes. He knew. "Maybe the hotel safe?" he asked. "Then we can meet Nellie at the pool and do something you'll think is really radical."

"Like what?"

Dan gave his crooked grin. "Have fun."

"Ah, Miss Cahill." The manager rose to greet her from his desk. He hurried to shake her hand. "I was so glad when you phoned. I knew your grandmother very well."

"You did?"

"Grace Cahill was a favorite guest for many years. She came first in the late forties and then just about every year for more than twenty years. We have hotel archives, and she's featured prominently."

"I didn't know that."

"Oh, yes. We have a wonderful photograph of your grandmother painting by the Nile. Would you like to see it?" He reached into his desk. "I tracked it down after you phoned."

Amy looked at the black-and-white photograph. Grace was younger and slimmer, wearing white trousers and a white shirt. A scarf was wrapped around her head. She was sitting at an easel somewhere in the gardens, facing the river. Next to her an older, stout man in a straw hat was painting the same scene.

"Isn't that . . ."

"Yes, Sir Winston Churchill, also a favorite guest. Prime Minister of Great Britain during World War Two, great statesman, all that. But also—did you know this?—a painter. He always told Grace she needed lessons from him. I believe this photograph was taken in the 1950s."

"Thank you for showing it to me. I was wondering if you'd keep something in the safe for me," Amy said, holding out the box with the Sakhet.

"Of course." He turned and opened the safe and placed the Sakhet inside. "And now, I must apologize to you for something." He took something else out of the safe. "Grace Cahill called us a year ago and asked us to track down a painting she had done and left as a gift. She wanted to buy it back. The manager before me had it hanging in his office for years. Then, after a renovation, it was misplaced. When she called, we searched and couldn't find it. Yet just today, when I went looking for this photograph, I found it. Now I'd like to present it to you as a gift, with the hotel's apologies." He handed her a small wrapped package.

Amy hugged it to her chest. "Thank you."

"You see?" Amy held out the painting to Dan. "Remember what Grace said in the card. *Don't forget the art!* Here it is!"

It was a watercolor of the Nile, and she recognized Grace's style as well as the view. She'd captured the spiky palms, the green water, the delicate legs of the sandpipers on the banks.

Dan sighed. "I have a feeling I'm not getting my swim."

Amy flipped the painting onto the bed. She bent back the nails that secured the painting to the frame. Dan watched as she carefully lifted off the backing and then lifted the painting out of the frame. "There's something not right about this."

Dan squinted at it. He took it and held it up to the light. "Look. Grace painted on the back of somebody else's painting."

Amy leaned closer to examine a scrawl at the bottom. "Grace painted on the back of *Winston Churchill*'s painting." She grinned. "This must be her revenge for him telling her that she needed art lessons from him."

"Amy, this was her revenge on a *Cahill*," Dan said. "Look at Churchill's painting. Do you see how the sunlight is all directed to one place? It's the island of Philae. See the Temple of Isis? This is the real island, before it was submerged."

"You're right! Churchill must have painted it as a hint toward the clue! I wonder which branch of the family he was in."

"I don't know, but if I had to guess, I'd bet he's a Lucian," Dan said. "He had that mastermind-of-destiny thing going on."

"I guess she painted over it to hide it," Amy said. She held the painting up again. "Wait a minute. Do you see these waves that Grace painted? What do they look like to you?" She pointed to waves, orange-tipped from the setting sun.

Dan looked for a long moment. "Arrows," he said. "They're *arrows.*"

"If you hold the painting up, you can see Churchill's painting of Philae. The arrows are pointing to that wall."

"The encircling arm!" Dan cried.

"This is a map," Amy said. "Pointing to Katherine's clue!"

"Great," Dan said in a defeated voice. "The clue is underwater. Maybe I *am* getting my swim. With the crocodiles. And those flesh-burrowing parasites."

Amy tapped her fingers on the desk. "There has to be a solution," she said.

Just then she noticed that the drawer to the desk was slightly open. She turned her head to the side and saw a small metal object inside.

Their room was bugged!

CHAPTER 21

The room door slammed. Nellie tossed her key on the dresser. "That pool is better than a chai smoothie. I am totally refreshed. Let me grab a shower and we'll discuss dinner plans. We only have one more evening in Aswan and I have some ideas."

Nellie stepped into the bathroom. Dan and Amy crowded in with her and closed the door.

"Guys? Uh, I know we've gotten close and all? But this is a *lit*-tle too much togetherness for me, 'kay?" Nellie said.

Amy reached over and turned on the shower full blast. "The hotel room is bugged," she said underneath the noise of the rushing water.

"Bugs in this hotel? Impossible. What is it, a spider or something? Chill out, I'll take care of it."

"Not bugs, *bugged*," Dan said. "As in, illegal surveillance."

"We need you to go out there and cover for us while we search for whoever's bugging us," Amy said. "Whoever it is, he or she is probably nearby."

"All you have to do is keep talking. We've thought a lot about this, and we think you have the necessary skills," Dan said.

"Very funny, Dan-o. But true. When it comes to non-stop chat, I'm the champ," Nellie agreed.

Nellie turned off the shower and they all returned to the main room. "That pool is so fine," she said, as if she'd never been interrupted. "I met this couple from Scotland, and I was all, whoa, you have some delish smoked salmon in your excellent country. . . ."

Amy raised the window carefully, not making a sound. She and Dan quietly climbed out.

"—and they were all, *'Aye, lassie, we dew, ye ken our bonny fish, ye dew!'*" Nellie said in a terrible Scottish accent. "So I said, 'You know what ye lads and lassies need in Scotland? Bagels! To go with!' *'Whoa,'* they said, *'lassie, ye canna be serious, that is one orrrig-in-al guid idea. . . .'*" With the drone of Nellie's Scottish burr in their ears, they hurried away.

Down the curving path, under the palms, past the gardens, and circling back to the front door of the hotel.

"I'm betting lobby," Dan said. "The device has a wireless transmitter, so we're going to have to examine everyone's ears."

"And how are we going to do that?"

"Say we're at a Q-Tip convention?"

They strolled inside. The lobby was crowded with guests taking shelter from the mid-afternoon heat.

Dan and Amy paused near a column and watched the crowd. At first it was hard to single any one person out. Tourists stood and sat and chatted, read guidebooks and magazines, passed each other newspapers, all taking a breather before the next round of temples.

Dan pointed with his chin to a man sitting with his back to them. He was a beefy guy in a stiff straw hat, a newspaper held up in front of his face. His thick neck was sunburned bright red. "He hasn't turned a page in five minutes. And he's got something in his ear. Come on."

"But I don't recognize him. . . ."

"I bet it's Eisenhower Holt in disguise."

Amy followed. Dan strode over to the man and ripped away the newspaper from in front of his face. "You're busted!"

"Just what do you think you are doing, sir?" the man blustered in a British accent.

Dan quickly handed him back his paper. "Uh, busted for wearing the best hat in the joint!" he said. "You rock!"

Amy tugged Dan away. "While you were assaulting that guy, everybody in the lobby looked up," she whispered. "Except *him*."

A man sat in the corner, a newspaper in front of his face. He was dressed in a suit the color of vanilla ice cream. Above the matching shoes, Dan glimpsed bright pink socks.

"That's him," Dan declared. "There's only one jerk we know who can conduct high-tech surveillance and accessorize at the same time."

He'd made a dumb joke, but it was only to cover up how crazy-mad he felt at the sight of his uncle. Alistair Oh had been the only Cahill to truly befriend them. At least, they'd thought so. Sure, they'd double-crossed each other a few times, but they'd also ended up working together. Alistair had saved their necks on more than one occasion. But he'd ended up being like the rest of the Cahills—out for himself and willing to betray anyone who got in his way.

Dan stalked over and grabbed a fistful of the newspaper, tearing it away from Alistair's face. "Surprise!"

Alistair Oh looked up at them sheepishly. "Greetings, young ones."

"Greetings, weasel," Dan said.

"Perhaps an explanation is in order—"

"Perhaps a whomp upside the head is in order," Dan said.

Amy took a few steps and reached for a house phone. She dialed their room number. When Nellie answered, she said, "Okay, you can stop now."

"Man, that's guid news," Nellie said. "This lassie is about to pass out."

Amy hung up the phone and turned back to Alistair. Dan faced their uncle, his arms crossed.

"I realize things look bad," Alistair said.

"Did you hear that?" Dan asked. "A dead man is talking."

"Amazing," Amy said. "But didn't you mean to say a lying, cheating, double-crossing dead man?"

"I had good reason for what I did!" Alistair exclaimed. "My safety depends on my being dead. Anything less wouldn't have worked. Do you see, our alliance will be stronger than ever."

"We don't *have* an alliance," Dan said. "Because you *lied.*"

"A small necessary deception. Think about it. Now I can operate undercover. You will have a truly silent partner. The Kabras think I'm dead. Soon the news will spread out to all Cahills."

"Your uncle thinks you're alive."

"Well." Alistair gave a slight cough. "He might have his reasons. But he won't tell the others. We are Ekats, no matter how we feel about each other."

"So why are you bugging our room?" Dan asked.

"I knew you'd talked to my uncle back in Cairo. I wanted to see if you'd made an alliance with him. You mustn't trust him."

"And we're supposed to trust *you*?" Amy asked scornfully.

"You bug us, and if you just happened to pick up information on a clue that you could beat us to, well, that would be a bonus, right?" Dan asked sarcastically.

"No, not beat you to it," Alistair said. "But help you, yes. We can do it together."

"We're supposed to believe you now?" Amy demanded. "We *trusted* you, Alistair. You *left* us."

Alistair sighed. He looked down and regarded his pink ankles. "I regret that you lost confidence in me," he said. He looked up and met their eyes. His warm brown gaze seemed sincere. "But I can't regret my actions. I did it for the best reasons. For our alliance."

"You keep using that word," Dan said. "Don't you get it? We don't trust weasels!"

"You must understand something," Alistair said. "This is just the beginning of the chase for the thirty-nine clues. There will be betrayals and seeming betrayals. There will be reversals. There will be victories that will turn out to be dust. What you must do is simple. No matter how things look, you must keep going. How do you do that? By following your heart. If you truly believe I'm not on your side, then walk away. But if you believe that together we can find this clue, then stay."

What should we do? Dan wondered. He was still furious at Alistair. They still felt rocky over the betrayal of Theo and Hilary. Maybe Amy was right—they couldn't trust anyone. Especially Alistair.

Except they were at a dead end, and they might need him.

"I have a way to find the clue," Alistair told them.

Dan shook his head. "No way."

Alistair smiled. "I am an Ekat. Way."

Alistair beat a path through the reeds with a stick. Mud soaked the bottoms of his cream-colored trousers, custom made for him by a very good tailor in Hong Kong. Sometimes sacrifice was necessary in pursuit of a worthy goal.

He had hired a taxi to take them south of the city, then dismissed the taxi at a Nubian village. He passed out bags of candy and pens in order to chase away the village boys clamoring for baksheesh. Now they were alone, on a dirt path to the river that had gradually grown more choked with weeds.

The surveillance device had maybe not been his best idea. He should have just knocked on the door and talked to them. But he couldn't be sure that they hadn't talked to Bae. He had to be certain they hadn't betrayed him.

That was the problem with all the Cahills — nobody knew how to trust. With good reason, of course. Alistair had betrayed and been betrayed more times than he could count.

He had wanted to escape the Cahill way. He had tried with Dan and Amy. But when he saw his chance to leave, pretend he was dead . . . he left them.

Sometimes sacrifice was necessary in pursuit of a worthy goal.

He told himself.

But there was a difference between trousers and children.

What was so sad was that he saw himself in them. His childhood had been sacrificed to the hunt for the Clues. His uncle had made sure of that. He had used Alistair's ingenuity, exploited it. Lied to him. Done unspeakable things in pursuit of a goal that eluded him. And now his uncle neared the end of his life and was even more desperate.

And Alistair was desperate now, too. Desperate to win. Because the 39 Clues could not fall into the hands of Bae Oh. Even though he was an Ekat.

What would happen to Dan and Amy? What would this chase do to them? What had Grace bequeathed them? *She should have protected them more,* Alistair thought with a flare of sorrow. Had the Clues corrupted her, too?

Was it up to him to protect them?

In that case, they were all in trouble. He would do the best he could, but he was no hero.

He could see by Dan's set face that the boy still didn't trust him. Alistair felt something strange touch his heart. *Affection.* An emotion he'd left behind so many years ago as he concentrated on the hunt for the Clues.

They burst through some underbrush and found themselves at the river. Alistair threw away the stick and pushed aside the reeds with his hands. "Behold," he said fondly. "The Ekat submersible."

Dan and Amy peered into the reeds. A small bubble-shaped craft sat on two legs that ended in what looked like oversize duck feet. The bubble was made of green-tinted plastic. There was a small propeller at one end.

"Are you kidding me?" Dan asked. "Did you buy that at Target?"

"I designed it myself," Alistair said, patting it.

Amy looked nervous. "Is there an escape hatch?"

"We don't need an escape hatch. It's a flawless design. You have the map?"

Amy nodded and pointed to her waist pack.

"It's the only way," Alistair said. "Philae is right out there waiting for us." He pointed to the green water. "And we don't have much daylight left."

"Dan?" Amy asked.

Dan looked out at the water. Alistair saw the boy calculate his chances, then throw them away. He would do it.

Was this a good trait or a dangerous one?

Nevertheless, Alistair's heart lifted as Dan nodded. "Let's go find a clue."

CHAPTER 22

The submersible plunged downward, and water closed over them. They glided deeper guided by a state-of-the-art (Alistair assured them) charting system. They all pressed forward in the small space, peering through the green, waiting to see the island appear. As the craft went deeper, the water grew more murky, dark and thick with silt.

"Hope we find it soon," Alistair said. "We don't want the oxygen to run out."

"Run out?" Dan asked. "I thought you said this was flawless."

"Well, yes, the design is. But not necessarily the air circulation. I didn't have time to completely perfect it." Alistair jerked the controls to keep the craft on course.

"Thanks for telling us!"

"Now, Dan, don't get excited. It uses too much oxygen."

"We'll try not to breathe," Amy muttered.

"I wasn't expecting these currents," Alistair said worriedly.

"Well, isn't *that* good news," Dan said.

The submersible was suddenly slammed by a current and spun sideways.

"Whoa," Alistair said, struggling for control. "There used to be rapids here, and waterfalls, before the dam, and I guess . . . there still are, just underneath the surface."

"Straight ahead!" Dan called. "I see it!"

The island suddenly appeared through the murky water, overgrown with aquatic plant life and the remnants of ancient walls. As Alistair piloted the craft closer, they struggled to match Grace's painting with what they saw. Alistair turned on an exterior light that illuminated the area around them.

"There," Alistair cried. "Do you see the rise? And that wall? That is where the Temple of Isis was! Can you see any distinguishing features from Grace's map?"

Amy moved the flashlight underneath the paper so that she could see both Churchill's painting and Grace's arrows. "See how the wall angles? And there are three large stones. One has a split down the middle."

"Can you get any closer?" Dan asked Alistair.

The craft lurched as it drifted closer. "It's hard . . . to keep . . . on course . . . ," Alistair said, struggling with the wheel. Suddenly, the craft zoomed ahead, pushed by a tricky current, and slammed into the wall. Amy gasped with alarm.

"It's all right, we're still airtight," Alistair said, checking the navigation lights. One began to blink yellow. "I think."

"Something's carved into the stone!" Dan suddenly cried. "Get closer!"

They peered through the murk as they bounced through turbulence. The submersible suddenly tumbled forward like a rolling ball, knocking Amy against the side. Her face pressed against the bubble, right against the ancient wall.

She could just make out two letters.

K.C.

"Katherine Cahill!" she shouted.

"I think the next one is numbers," Dan said. "Get closer!"

"I see it!" Amy cried.

Alistair maneuvered the craft closer. Fronds waved in front, carried by the current, and they had to wait until their view cleared. The light shone on the wall.

1/2 gm M

"One half of a gram!" Dan said.

"But what's with the M and Ms?" Amy asked.

"Yeah, I prefer Skittles," Dan said, peering at the wall.

There was a sharp cut in the stone after the large M. "It looks like the big M is covering another letter," Amy said. "There must have been a word there. We can't read it!"

"It must have happened when they moved the temple," Dan said.

There was a sheen of sweat on Alistair's face. "No," he said quietly. "The M is for Madrigal. They did it."

As if pushed by an unseen hand, the submersible suddenly rocked from side to side alarmingly. Amy and Dan grabbed the edges of their seats as Alistair struggled for control. Suddenly, a red light began to blink on the console.

"We're taking on water," Alistair said. "There must be a leak. If the submersible gets too heavy . . ."

"What?" Amy asked frantically.

"We can't rise."

Alistair yanked the controls. "The water must have gotten in the electrical system. I lost the rudder!"

The current picked up the submersible like a small stick and hurled it toward the wall.

"Do something!" Dan cried.

"I'm trying!"

Terror plastered Amy to her seat. At the very last moment, the current whirled the submersible away.

"What are we going to do?" Amy tried to keep the panic out of her voice. Trapped under the deep waters of the lake, and nobody knew where they were . . .

It was as though the malevolent force of the Madrigals had worked on them from afar and led them to their doom.

Alistair looked at the gauges. His face grew pale. "We're sinking."

Amy gripped the sides of her chair. Slowly, the submersible sank to the bottom. It bumped down on the sand and tilted to one side. Everything went silent.

Was this how it would end, with this terrible silence?

"How much air do we have?" Amy asked.

Alistair looked at the gauge. "Difficult to say."

She looked at him hard. "Say it."

He swallowed. "Fifteen minutes. Maybe."

They were all silent for a long moment. Then Dan shook his head.

"No," he said firmly. "No way. I'm not giving up. We're getting out of here."

Alistair clicked on several buttons. "I'm sorry . . . there's no electrical power at all. There's nothing we can do."

"Look up ahead," Dan urged. "See where the bottom drops off? You can actually *see* the current. It's wicked fast. If we could catch it . . ."

Ahead, Amy saw a ripple of water, a gleam of green, like a channel cutting through the murk. "I see it," she said. "But how do we get to it?"

"We walk," Dan said, turning to Amy. "Remember? At the fairground I won the race . . ."

"The bubble race!" Amy exclaimed. "Let's try it!"

Alistair watched in confusion as the two of them threw their weight against the front of the bubble-shaped craft. It started to roll forward slowly. They took another step, and it rolled forward again, another inch.

"I've got it!" Alistair said. He sprang up and joined in.

Inch by agonizing inch, slipping and sliding into each other, they rolled the bubble over the bottom, closer and closer to the current.

"Just . . . a . . . few . . . more feet . . . ," Dan said, sweat pouring down his face.

They strained with all their might. The submersible bumped off the drop-off, hit the current, and shot forward.

Now they were caught in a screaming current, jouncing along at a rapid pace.

"Woo-hoo!" Dan screamed as they zoomed along.

They held on as it bounced and revolved, completely at the mercy of the rushing water. Amy slammed her head against the roof. Alistair clung to his seat.

"It's bringing us to shallow water!" Dan cried.

They could see the bottom of the lake rising to meet them. With a sudden *whoosh,* they bounced against the ground and popped up above the surface. Water lapped around their sneakers, but the thing still floated.

Alistair reached over and released the hatch. "I have a pair of oars," he said sheepishly.

"Great," Dan said as they bobbed in the river. "A green bubble being rowed down the Nile. This shouldn't attract any attention at all."

Luck was like Halloween candy, Dan reflected. Sure, you got to feast on Milky Ways for awhile, but before you knew it, you were scraping the bottom of the plastic pumpkin, and the only thing left was a lone piece of candy corn with fuzz on it.

Then you bit it, and it broke your tooth.

The shadows lengthened outside the Old Cataract Hotel as they stood saying good-bye to Alistair. Defeat was etched on their faces. They'd almost died, and they still hadn't found the Clue. It was lost forever, stolen by the Madrigals.

Alistair bowed. "I apologize for almost drowning you," he said. "Grace would have been furious. I can hear her voice saying, *Alistair, there are calculated risks, and then there is overconfidence.*"

"Where are you going next?" Dan asked him.

"First, back home, to my library," Alistair said. "When you hit a dead end, more research can sometimes be the answer."

Amy felt that way, too. But in this case, she didn't know what to research. She'd failed. She only knew she was too tired to take another step.

"I'm flying to Cairo tonight for a connecting flight to Seoul," he said. "I'll give you my new cell number. Memorize it, please—don't write it down."

He passed along a slip of paper. Dan glanced at it, then tore it up.

"Are you sure you memorized it?"

Dan gave him a *you've got to be kidding me* look.

Alistair chuckled. "Let me tell you something—you two have unique talents. In the beginning, I thought you'd be completely outclassed. How wrong I was. If you need a place to stay in Cairo, feel free to use my card at the Hotel Excelsior. I've received word that my uncle has returned to Seoul. You'll be safe there for a night or two."

"What about the other Ekats?" Amy asked.

"Oh, don't worry—nobody goes there. Everyone got sick of Bae telling them what a genius he was to put it together, and how stupid they were not to realize it. So you might say there's a boycott. Everyone prefers the Bermuda Triangle, anyway—now, there's a stronghold!"

Dan gulped. He'd like to explore this whole Bermuda Triangle idea, but Amy had that look on her face, like she was already planning the next step. Missing the cool stuff on the way, as usual.

Amy nodded. "Good idea," she said. "We need a place to plan our next move."

"I've received word that the Holts are operating somewhere near St. Petersburg," Alistair said. "That's an option, though the odds of the Holts doing something intelligent are very low."

"Thanks for the tip," Dan said. "I think we'll skip it."

"That's probably wise," Alistair said. He sighed. "The chances of finding a clue left untouched by an original Cahill . . . well, it was a dream, wasn't it? Now we know that there's a half gram of . . . something waiting for us to discover." He gave them a small salute. "See you out there."

Amy and Dan walked slowly back to the hotel room, too depressed to speak.

"I don't know what else to do," Amy burst out finally. "We almost *died* down there! How could she have led us there like that?"

"She didn't know that the Madrigals would cut away the stone," Dan said.

"Even so," Amy said. "How could she think we'd be able to get under that deep water?"

Dan gripped Amy's arm. "Wait a second. Maybe she didn't. Remember you said that Grace had tried to get the painting back? Maybe she didn't *want* us to find it. Maybe it's an *old* hint. She painted it before the second dam."

"You could be right," Amy said as she unlocked the door. "Maybe *that's* why I don't remember any notes in the guidebook for Aswan. Because there *weren't* any. Grace told us to follow in her footsteps, but *we're* the ones who figured out the Isis clue. Then *Hilary* told us to come here. Probably because she had a plan to steal the Sakhet."

Dan took out Grace's card and read it again. "We're missing something."

Amy hung over his shoulder. Then she put her finger on a sentence. "Look at this, Dan."

If only I'd been __half__ the grandmother I should have been

"The word *half* is underlined. And the 'g' in *grandmother* is darker than the rest of the word."

"One half gram," Dan said with a groan. "It was there all the time. We didn't have to come here at all. But we're still left with the most important question. *Half gram of what?*"

"This is so frustrating! We're just one step behind her."

"As usual." Dan frowned. "If we shouldn't have come to Aswan, I say we go back to Cairo."

"Let's pack," Amy agreed.

They began to throw things into their duffels and backpacks. Dan held up the gold-painted base from the Sakhet. "Trash or save?"

"Trash," Amy said. "It's worthless."

Dan tossed it in the wastebasket. It flipped over and landed bottom up. "Hey, Amy. C'mere."

Amy sighed and went over. "Trash in a trash can. Color me stunned."

"Look at the label. Treasures of Egypt. This came from a shop in Cairo. Here's the name and address. It's in the Citadel, whatever that is."

"So? Grace bought it there."

"Why did Grace buy a base for the Sakhet? To conceal it, Hilary said. But it's been in a safety deposit box for what, thirty years?"

"Grace's message!" Amy exclaimed. "End with the *basics,* she said. Could she have meant this?"

"It's our only lead," Dan said. "We've got to follow in her footsteps — back in Cairo."

CHAPTER 23

"'The Citadel was first used for defense,'" Amy said, reading aloud from the new guidebook. "'Now it has many holy sites. It offers some of the best views of the city.'"

"It also has a bunch of streets with no signs," Dan said, looking around. "How are we going to find this shop?"

"With great difficulty, obviously," Amy answered, consulting the map.

They walked through the twisting streets and alleys of the Citadel for twenty minutes. Finally, they found themselves in an unmarked alley. Most of the signs were in Arabic. There were no numbered addresses.

"Never mind how we're going to find it, how did *Grace* find it?" Dan wondered.

Amy stopped in front of a narrow doorway that appeared like all the others. The window was dark. It looked closed. "This is it."

"You sure?"

"I'm sure. Look."

Dan's photographic memory clicked in. "It's just like Grace's card. Treasures, Egypt, and welcome were all in a line going down."

Amy clutched his arm. "She led us here, Dan. This is it!"

Amy pushed open the door, and a bell tinkled. The shop was long and narrow, its shelves crowded with pottery and metalwork. Rugs covered the floor. In the very back, she could see a man sitting at a counter reading a book. He looked up at her for a moment.

"You are welcome to look around." He looked back down at his book.

That was weird. She'd never been anywhere in Egypt where someone wasn't eager to sell her something, pressing close, offering her bargains and cups of tea.

"Excuse me?" Dan walked forward. "Did you sell this item?" He placed the base on the desk.

The man picked it up. He was a handsome young Egyptian dressed in a snowy white shirt and a striped scarf that he'd wrapped around his neck despite the heat. He gave the base a quick glance. "Hard to say," he said. "It looks like something we would use to showcase a souvenir. I can show you some just like it."

"We don't want another one," Amy said. "We want to know if you remember this one."

"I am sorry." He looked at her for the first time, and he must have caught her frustration. "I am not sure what you are asking."

"Do you remember meeting a woman called Grace Cahill?"

The man shook his head. "I know no one by that name."

Amy and Dan exchanged a glance. *Now or never.* Grace had led them here for a reason. Dan slipped the Sakhet out of his backpack. Amy had given it to him to carry. "Have you ever seen this?"

Dan saw recognition in his eyes, but he quickly shook his head. "No."

"We're Grace Cahill's grandchildren," Dan said. "We believe she sent us here."

He looked at them for a long moment. His gaze was searching and somehow honest. Then he leaned forward. "That is a beautiful necklace, miss."

"Thank you."

"Thirty years ago, the clasp broke. May I?" His fingers reached out and touched the clasp gently.

"My father repaired it. I'm glad to see it is still intact."

"So you *do* know her."

"Forgive me for my hesitation. One must be careful. My name is Sami Kamel. Please call me Sami."

"I'm Amy, and this is Dan."

"So you've come at last." He left his chair at the counter and went to the door. He flipped the sign to CLOSED.

"Please. If you would come with me." He bowed slightly, then moved a curtain and disappeared.

Amy and Dan followed him into a small, cozy room. He directed them to sit and then poured them mint tea in fragile porcelain cups.

"Your grandmother knew my father," he said. "And my father's father. My father's father was a famous . . . how can I say this . . . crook."

Amy and Dan laughed a little, startled.

"But a good man," Sami went on with a smile. "A forger of antiquities. He did a favor for your grandmother in the late forties, he would never say what. When my father took over the business in 1952, he convinced my grandfather to retire the, uh, illegitimate part of his business. We sell some good items, some high-quality, some cheap, but our customers always know what they are getting. Your grandmother came to the shop on every visit to Egypt. She was great friends with my grandfather and my father."

Amy took a sip of tea. "You said, 'you've come at last.'"

"Your grandmother told my father that you would be coming. He has been keeping something for her for some time now. She bought it on her last trip to Cairo. And now, I give it to you."

He spun on his chair and reached out to the bookcases behind him. He flipped a lever concealed in the wood molding and the books revolved. He withdrew an old wooden game board and placed it on the tea table. "This."

"She left us a game of checkers?" Dan asked.

Sami smiled. "Not checkers. Senet. It's an ancient Egyptian game. A number of sets have been found in tombs, but no rules have survived. This one is not that old, but it is beautiful. Mother-of-pearl inlay and carved wood. We think it once had valuable marking pieces, perhaps made of gold, because there was originally a key to lock this drawer, where the pieces were kept."

"A drawer?" Amy reached out but he held up a hand.

"Wait. Your grandmother had my father fashion another lock for the drawer. See the letters? He used what the Chinese would call an alphabet lock. Only a password will open it. You have to click the letters into place."

"We don't have a password," Dan said. "If we try some things . . ."

"You only get one chance," Sami said. "It is the safeguard that you are who you say you are. If you don't get it, the drawer will not open at all. You can smash the game board, but there are two problems. One, it would destroy what was inside. Two, I would not allow you to do it. That is my order." He smiled at them, but they saw resolve behind the smile.

Dan and Amy looked at each other, stricken. They had no idea what to try.

"My father said that Grace was sure you would know."

"Did she . . . say anything that might give us a clue?" Amy asked.

"I am sorry. Just that you would know for certain."

He withdrew a little further away to give them privacy. Amy pressed her fingers against her forehead.

"Well, I *don't* know," she murmured. "It could be so many things."

"What do people usually use for passwords?" Dan said. "Their middle name? Where they were born? Or Grace's favorite color — green. Or her favorite ice cream . . ."

"Pistachio."

"Favorite food . . ."

"Sushi. Favorite place . . ."

"'Sconset in August, Paris at Christmas, New York in the fall, Boston anytime," Dan recited.

They both knew Grace's favorites by heart. Those weren't just *words* to them, Amy suddenly thought. They were memories.

Amy recognized something then. All this time, memory after memory had filled in the blank shape where Grace had been. Sitting on the steps of a museum, waving hot pretzels. Baking brownies. Getting a giggling fit in a library, listening to Grace spin a tale by a roaring fire. Jumping into the cold ocean. Running down a Boston street in the rain.

"I was wrong," she said, leaning in to Dan. "I was *so* wrong. I didn't trust my memories. Grace *did* prepare us for this, but not out of some warped power trip. She prepared us out of *love*. She knew what was in store. And she knew we couldn't escape it. There's a reason she wanted us in this race for the clues. We don't know it yet. But we have to trust her. I mean, *really* trust her. Stop second-guessing her. We have to let her back in."

"It's hard not to be mad at her when I miss her so much," Dan said.

"We can be mad that she's gone. Just plain furious. But not at *her*."

Suddenly, Dan smiled. Something settled inside both of them, fitting like a puzzle piece. Amy felt the satisfying *click*.

Dan nodded. "Okay. Back to the problem. She'd know that we'd go through everything we could think of. It has to be not a *guess*, but an absolutely sure thing." Dan paced the room, trying to think. A large portrait hung over a desk, and its eyes seemed to be following him. It was a painting of an old man with a long white beard and piercing dark eyes.

"Friend of yours?" he asked Sami.

"Not really. It's Salah ad-Din. A famous Muslim commander who built the Citadel back in 1176. You Americans would call him—"

Amy and Dan said the word together in one long *aha* exhalation. "Saladin."

"Exactly."

Amy brought the game board closer. She looked up at Dan. He nodded.

She moved the letters in the lock one by one.

They gasped as the lid popped open.

"You see?" Sami smiled. "You know your grandmother better than you think."

Amy looked at Dan. "Yes," she said softly. "We do."

Sami gave a short bow. "I will leave you to examine what she's left."

They waited until the curtain was drawn. Amy slid the drawer open. She took out a small drawing in a linen mat.

"It looks like a botanical illustration," she said.

"There's something written in pencil," Dan said.

mat 2.11

"Looks like the price of the mat," Amy said.

"All we have to do," Dan said, "is figure out what plant this leaf belongs to, and we have the clue."

"That shouldn't be too hard," Amy said.

CHAPTER 24

"This is all your fault," Dan said to Amy back in the Hotel Excelsior. "Don't you know by now that you can never, ever say that something is going to be *easy*?"

Amy dropped her head in her hands. "I know."

"Try chervil," Nellie suggested. She leaned over to feed Saladin another blob of hummus. They had ordered room service just for him to thank him for being such an awesome password.

Dan sat hunched over his laptop. He'd found an online dictionary of botanical illustrations, but it proved harder than they'd expected to match a leaf to a species. And it didn't help that Nellie kept throwing out random herbs, as if she were making a stew.

"How many entries are there?" Amy asked him.

"Sheesh, I don't know. Thousands."

"And since we've been here, how many entries have you checked?"

Dan looked down at the list he was compiling. "Thirty-seven. No! Thirty-eight. I forgot chervil."

Amy groaned. "We've been here for twenty minutes. This could take all night."

"And tomorrow," Nellie said. "Try tamarind!"

Dan clicked away. "No," he said, disappointed.

Amy sprang up. She paced in back of Dan. "That's an idea, though," she said. "I mean, here we are in Egypt. We should look up Egyptian plants. Katherine wouldn't lead all her descendants here for chervil, would she?"

"Try acacia," Nellie suggested.

"Or hummus, or baba ghanoush, or mint, or palm." Dan spun around in the desk chair, waving his arms. "My brain is on overload."

"This place can do that to you," Nellie agreed. "We saw so much in a few days. Temples and tombs and ancient cities. Amazing sunsets, beautiful art—"

"Sure, but you're leaving out the coolest stuff," Dan said. "Crocodiles, pharaoh curses, brain hooks, body parts in canopic jars—what's not to like?"

"I liked seeing those old photos of Grace," Amy said. "Remember the goofy one of her at Hatshepsut's Temple? Sometimes I forget how funny she was."

"Pretzels and mustard," Dan said. "Remember? She used to say, *Pay attention! Everything counts!*"

Dan appreciated the little things, just like Grace, Amy thought. She remembered the day they'd first arrived at this suite. How he'd run around the rooms, calling out every object with delight, like he'd never seen it before. *Pillows! Bible! Robes! Shampoo!*

"People say I look like Grace," Amy said. "But you're the one who's like her."

Dan shrugged and turned back to the computer. Amy saw that the tips of his ears were glowing red, a sure sign that she'd pleased him. She could have said *I'm sorry.* She could have said *You were right. I wanted Grace's memory for myself.* But she knew she'd said enough.

"Everything counts," Amy murmured. She gazed at the image on Grace's card, the Magi arriving to bring gifts to the Christ child, looking way more fat and regal than any newborn Amy had ever seen.

Suddenly, words and images became a mash-up in her head.

Magi. Hatshepsut. Punt.

Even back in the New Kingdom, a queen had to go Christmas shopping.

As if in a trance, Amy slid open the bedside drawer. She took out the Bible Dan had found. She flipped rapidly through the pages to Matthew, chapter two, verse eleven.

"Dan?" she asked in a voice that trembled a little. "Look up myrrh. M-y-r-r-h," she spelled out, coming to stand behind him. Nellie hurried over.

Dan typed out the word in the search engine. The leaf flashed on screen.

MYRRH

Pronunciation: [mur]
Latin: Commiphora myrrha

see also "Sweet Cicely"

myrrh

"That's it!" Dan cried. "Now explain how you did that."

"*Don't forget the art.* We thought it was her painting, but we figured out that Grace *didn't* leave that as a clue. We forgot to think about what she really meant." Amy held up the card. "She was talking about the card itself."

"I still don't get it."

"It all has to do with Hatshepsut."

"Hatshepsut?" Nellie looked puzzled. "But she lived thousands of years before Christmas was around."

"Hatshepsut went to the Land of Punt and came back with myrrh trees. Grace posed right in front of that relief. And she made that joke in the guidebook about how a queen has to go *Christmas* shopping? She was leading us back to this." Amy held up the card. "The *Magi.* They brought—"

"Gifts to the Christ child," Nellie said.

Amy picked up the Bible. "Matthew, chapter two, verse eleven. Mat 2:11 is a notation, not the price of the mat around the drawing. Listen." Amy read the verse out loud. "'And when they had opened their treasures, they presented gifts to him; gold, frankincense, and myrrh.'"

Dan nodded. "And Grace misspelled 'resonates.' Grace was an excellent speller—we should know. We played Scrabble with her every weekend for *years*. Myrrh is a *resin*! A half gram of myrrh. That's the clue!"

Amy's eyes shone. "And Grace was with us all the way. She didn't abandon us, Dan. She'll help us when we need it. And it will be just like her, too. It won't be when we expect it. It'll be when we *least* expect it. She hasn't gone away. She's still with us."

Dan turned away from her. But Amy knew it was because his eyes had filled. Her eyes were full of tears, too. She felt as though Grace's hand was on her shoulder, squeezing. Saying *good work, Amy.*

Grace had come back to them. They would never lose her again.

Suddenly, they heard a noise from next door. A muffled thump.

"That came from the stronghold," Dan said in a low tone.

"Should we look?" Amy asked.

"Maybe it's Alistair," Nellie said.

They all crept to the connecting door. They put their ears against it.

"I don't hear anything," Amy whispered.

"I think we should check it out," Dan said.

He got the umbrella from the closet, unscrewed the handle, and fitted it into the lock. The knob turned.

He opened it in an inch and put his eye to the crack.

"What do you see?" Amy whispered.

"Wonderful things," Dan said. "On the floor."

He pushed open the door. The stronghold had been violated. Vitrines were smashed, paintings thrown, panels tossed. They walked through carefully, avoiding the shattered glass.

The Sakhets were gone, the pedestals empty.

"Who could have done this?" Amy whispered.

Nellie bent down to pick up something off the floor. A scrap of black cloth, probably torn off by the protruding edge of a shattered vitrine.

Amy looked at the design woven into the cloth. She realized that the pattern was a repeating letter. M.

Fear clutched her heart. "Madrigals," she whispered.